SOME CALL IT LOVE

A SWEET DREAMS NOVEL

SARAH PEIS

Some Call It Love

Published by Hexatorial
Developmental Editing: Natasha Orme
Copy Editing: Hot Tree Editing
ISBN ebook 978-0-6481085-0-4
ISBN print 978-0-6481085-4-2

DEDICATION

To cupcakes

PROLOGUE

"You're under arrest. You have the right to remain silent. Anything you say .... Gun! Gun!"

What started out as a terrible day just got a whole lot worse. Who would have thought that I'd find myself squashed to the asphalt by an overweight, sweaty police officer who thought I was hiding a gun in the pocket of my pants? The same guy who used to copy my history notes all through high school now acted like I was a dangerous criminal, when he very well knew that I have never even so much as stolen a pen in my life.

"Ray, it's not a gun. It's—" I stopped myself midsentence. Maybe it was better if he did think I had a gun. If he found out what was actually in my pocket, my humiliation would be complete. I knew waking up in a bed that wasn't my own this morning was bad luck. It threw my zen off and look what happened. I was getting arrested for something that was entirely not my fault. Well, almost entirely. My bike didn't smash into him by itself, but it was extenuating circumstances and my actions were entirely justified. I was getting arrested for a simple misunderstanding.

Of course, Officer Ray, as he insisted I call his judgmental ass, reached into my pocket to investigate and pulled out a bright pink dildo. It was new, too. My best friend, Maisie, got it for my last birthday. Since I hadn't retired good ole Bob, I hadn't even used this one yet.

"Everyone stand down. No gun, just a vibrator," the bastard called out to his colleagues who stared, then laughed louder than necessary. To make my humiliation complete, said bastard started waving the vibrator above his head. "If you were that desperate, you could have just called me."

Did I mention that Ray was also a sleazy slimeball? He stood me back up, my hands now cuffed behind my back and his hands on my butt. By tomorrow everyone and their mother would know about this. He was a gossip queen, and his followers were vast and quick to spread the news. In other words, I was screwed. I could never show my face at the QuickMart down the road again. I should start mourning the loss of the slushies I used to get there.

Make one bad decision, and your reputation is ruined. Okay, maybe a few bad decisions. But everyone's been there. Nobody's perfect, right? Things happen. You move on.

But I should probably start where it all began. When the life I more or less loved came crashing down around me and I found myself face-to-face with my destiny—my very hot and very lickable destiny. Jameson Drake. I should have known to run the second he set his sights on me. After all, he was named after a drink that gave me terrible hangovers.

It should also be noted here that I would never lick any part of Jameson ever again. Only if he asked me to. Maybe begged me a little. Without a shirt on.

1

The first time I made eye contact with Jameson was from across a crowded club. My eyes went wide, and my jaw dropped as soon as I looked into his mesmerizing orbs of perfection. The details are a bit hazy because my brain refused to function other than to tell my eyes to open and close in rapid succession. Since I wasn't drinking and didn't approach strangers—stranger danger, right?—I forced myself to look away and get on with my life. Magical moment over, or so I thought.

"Willa? Are you still with us?" Maisie said while she waved her hand in front of my face. "I think she's gone into a sugar coma." She turned to the other part of our trio, Stella. "I told her not to drink Coke. She can't handle all that caffeine and sugar. It's the combination of death."

I blinked a few times and studied my shoes. Or more accurately, my kick-ass stilettos that cost me three months of extra shifts at the Donut Hole. But they were worth every cent. The dress I wore was short, shorter than I was used to, and tight, tighter than I would ever wear. It was also blue. But somehow, my two best friends had talked me into letting my hair down for one night, and apparently that meant dressing like a hooker—except for the shoes, because they were all class.

I rolled my eyes at Maisie and flicked her ear. "Stop talking about me like I'm not here. And I can handle my sugar and caffeine just fine."

They both laughed at me and ordered another drink. We all knew that I definitely was not able to handle sugar or caffeine. The effects were varied and unpredictable. I resentfully pushed the glass of water that Maisie had gotten me out of the way.

"Did you hand in your sociology report yet?" Stella asked. We all went to Winchester University. Maisie and I had been inseparable ever since bonding over our shared love of chocolate milk in first grade. Stella, Maisie's roommate, moved to Humptulips to go to the university since she lived on a farm in the middle of nowhere.

I stayed around because I couldn't leave my dad unless I was willing to risk him living in a jail cell for the rest of his life. And that was the best-case scenario. Let's just say Garret Montgomery did whatever Garret Montgomery wanted to do, even if it included stealing a cop car to get smokes from the gas station down the road.

Maisie used to be engaged to Ray, a local cop who absolutely saw no reason to leave his cushy job behind and move to another city. The crime rate in Humptulips was made up of 80 percent jaywalking and 20 percent whatever shit my dad came up with. So she stayed, went to school, and got ready for her life as a devoted housewife once she graduated. That was until she saw her darling husband-to-be getting too friendly with one of the Bennet twins. She packed her bags faster than you can say pineapple upside-down cake and moved in with Stella.

Stella was the balance to our crazy, the only person who could talk us off the ledge. And, yes, there might have been an actual ledge involved at one time.

I shook my head at Stella's question about the report, but Maisie nodded. "That would be a yes for me and a no for Willa." I knew she would have finished the report a week before it was due.

I pouted at her statement even though that's what my usual MO was when it came to homework. Why do it today when you can procrastinate and write it the day it's due?

"At least I started my research. Writing about the evolution of Thor as part of Norse mythology is harder than I thought. I was a bit hasty making my decision based on the movie and Chris Hemsworth's abs. Most of the literature is written in Old Norse, and I have to find translations. It's taking forever."

I groaned at the thought of the paper I had to write in less than a week. This one was definitely not last-minute kind of work, and I had to keep up my grades to stay eligible for my scholarship. I had done surprisingly well so far, but this class was turning me into a fruit loop. Apparently everyone had to take classes outside of their chosen major, but I was stupid enough to choose something that required hours of research.

"Holy smokes, do you see that guy?" Stella asked, attempting to nod her head inconspicuously but failing miserably. Maisie took a sip of her drink, following Stella's line of sight and promptly choked on it. "Is that Jameson?"

Maisie narrowed her eyes and nodded. "Definitely Jameson. Don't get too close or you might get pregnant." I should also mention that Maisie was a judgmental bitch at times. This was one of those times. "Remember Hannah?"

Of course I remembered Hannah. She tried to be the one to tie down Jameson by proclaiming to everyone and their mother that she was pregnant with his baby. Of course, she wasn't, because if we knew anything about Jameson it was that he was careful when it came to protecting his independence, and a baby was the last thing he wanted.

The truth came out eventually but not before she'd already done a lot of damage.

I knew Jameson couldn't keep it in his pants, but nobody deserved to be treated that way. And the gossip mill was still going strong, not letting anyone forget about the incident. It was, after all, one of the most exciting things to happen to this town since Barry Laker painted his house blue.

I stole a glance over Stella's shoulder and looked straight at none other than tall, dark, and broody. I was confused as to why he would be watching us. In all the years we had lived in the same town, he had exchanged exactly three words with me, three words I would always remember. His deep baritone gave me shivers, and looking at his eyes made me lose all brain function.

Word one was to order a Coke, word two to order a burger, and word three was to ask me for the bill. And I'm not even kidding when I say it was a total of three words. He didn't do polite, and he certainly didn't waste his words. He believed in the power of one-word communication.

Maisie nudged me and nodded toward him much more subtly than Stella. "He is definitely watching, and I am pretty sure it's you he's looking at."

I tried hard not to turn my head again and glued my eyes to Maisie instead. "I don't think so. But I have to head off now anyway. You guys want a lift?"

Stella was talking to someone we knew from class, and if the gleam in her eyes was anything to go by, also her latest hookup.

"I'm good. Lance is around here somewhere, so I'll just catch a ride with him later," Maisie said.

"If you're sure," I said, knowing the crush Maisie had on her brother's friend all too well. Maisie waved me off when I did my duty as devoted friend and asked her again if she wanted to come with me. After a round of hugs and promises to meet up the next day, she pushed her way through the mass of people.

I made it outside after receiving a few slaps to the ass, and someone was even so nice as to share their drink with me. The top half of my dress now had a big wet spot down the front, making it look like my tits were leaking. There weren't many people around, and the fresh air made me breathe easier again. At least I could start my paper early in the morning and maybe have something to show Maisie. I knew she would be on me again tomorrow.

I walked the few blocks to my car and shivered in my thin dress. It was hard to find free parking near the club, and I wasn't picky where I parked as long as it didn't cost me anything, a decision I regretted in moments like these when I turned onto the dark side street. At least my car was still there. It wouldn't be the first time someone broke into it or towed it, leaving me with no way to get back home.

I unlocked the door, thinking about the leftover pizza in my fridge. Lost in thought, I didn't hear someone approaching until they were next to me, making me jump back in surprise and emit a loud squeal.

The guy put up his hands to indicate he meant no harm, and I immediately recognized Jameson.

"Willa," he said in his raspy voice.

I stepped back to put some distance between us. "How do you know my name?"

Very smooth, Willa. Just blurt out the first stupid thing that comes to mind.

"Of course I know your name. We went to school together." Holy caboodle, that was one long-ass sentence for him. Was he drunk?

Okay, now I was ready to get my camera out to document this pivotal moment in my life. The moment the mighty Jameson talked to me. With my luck, I should have really known better than to assume he just came out to corner me in a dark alley to have a chat.

I blamed it on his eyes. They sucked you in and didn't let go. My brain function shut down, and I think I could feel a little drool on the corner of my mouth. Not my finest moment.

When I stayed quiet and stared at him open-mouthed, he took that as an invitation to continue. "Look, your dad owes me a lot of money. He's not settling his debt, and he put you down as his reserve, so to speak. If he can't pay, it's your debt."

My dream where he came out here to declare his undying love for me came crashing down. Unicorns were crying rainbow tears, and kittens wailed in agony. I should have known better than to assume he was interested in me.

So I yelled. Because it seemed appropriate. And besides, when I'm upset, I yell. It's never healthy to keep your emotions locked up tight. That shit could give you cancer. Or an ulcer. "Are you fucking kidding me?" I had definitely found my voice again. "I didn't lose that money, and I have no intention of paying it back."

"I don't think you understand how this works."

"And I don't think you understand how impossible it is for me to pay off any debt my dad might have with you." I stupidly decided this was a good point in our conversation to poke him in the chest to accentuate each word.

My finger just wouldn't stop poking once it made contact with his firm pecks. Holy hotness, he was built. My out-of-control finger wandered down and hit his abs, and they were just as firm. I was pretty sure that was an eight-pack I was poking.

Before I could travel further south, he caught my finger and held on tight.

"I want my money, Willa. $20k is not something I can just brush off."

When I heard the number, my eyes went wide and I was pretty sure they were bulging out of my head. "$20K? $20K? Twenty fucking grand?"

"It's not gonna get any less the more you repeat the number." The bastard looked amused, yet there was nothing amusing about this situation.

I pulled my finger from his hand, already lamenting the moment he wasn't touching me anymore. My finger was one lucky bitch.

"I know that, jackass." Oh no, I can't believe that just came out of my mouth. *Bad mouth.*

"I think it's a safe bet to say that you don't have the money. I hope you know what you're doing because this is one situation you can't get out of simply by blinking your big eyes and showing off your tits."

I narrowed aforementioned eyes and pushed at his

chest in anger. "And I think it's safe to say that you're an ass. I don't have the money that I don't owe you."

He leaned in until we were nose to nose. "Do you think you are the first one to tell me that they can't pay me? So let's skip the bullshit. I want my money, so find a way to get it to me."

I took a deep breath and regretted it immediately when his scent filled my nose. He was still entirely too close, and his big, stupid arms caged me in, making escape impossible. I also didn't think my feet would work at this stage. They seemed to like him just as much as my finger and inched closer instead of retreating.

"I don't have your money. My bank balance shows $4.37 at the moment. You know why I know that? Because I just had to pay the rent, which means I'm broke until I get paid next week. And it certainly won't be twenty grand they'll pay me." I turned my head to avoid breathing him in again but didn't quite succeed since he was so close. "And I would appreciate it if you could take a step back and stop harassing me."

Instead of doing what he was told, he stepped closer until all of him touched all of me. Dear donut gods, please make this stop.

My knees were ready to give up holding my body, and my hands went on another quest. I meant to push him away, but the second they made contact it was all over. Just like my finger, they refused to let go.

Jameson wasn't impressed with my refusal to pay. Well tough titties, because there was no way I could get that much money.

He was still leaning in too close and said, "I don't think you grasp the gravity of the situation, sweetheart."

My mouth was still going strong, refusing to give up the fight even though the rest of my body had. "Oh, I get the gravity just fine. But what you don't seem to grasp is that you can't squeeze money out of someone who has less than five dollars in her bank account."

He studied my face and took a step back. The relieved exhale that came out of my mouth would be heard by the rats in the sewers two counties over.

"I want the money by tomorrow."

"What? Are you crazy? How do you think I can come up with twenty grand in twenty-four hours?" I motioned to my beat-up old Ford. "Does this scream money to you?"

"That's not my problem." He held out his hand. "Give me your phone."

I pulled my bag closer. "No way. I'm not giving you anything."

He sighed and took the bag out of my hands. I was too stunned at his audacity to hold onto it. After a quick search, he came up with my phone, and I had to admit I was slightly impressed. It took me a lot longer to find anything in the endless depths of my key-swallowing bag. He typed something in and handed it back to me. "My number, so we can set up a time and place to meet."

And with that he was gone. If only I knew at that moment that my life had just taken a tumble down the rabbit hole.

2

I WOKE UP HAVING SLEPT VERY LITTLE AND NO CLOSER TO getting the money than I was the night before. After tossing and turning for most of the night, I gave up and stumbled out of bed bleary eyed before it was even light outside.

This was unheard of. On my rare days off from the Sweet Dreams bakery, I would sleep until noon. I usually worked there from four in the morning until around ten. So a lie-in was an absolute treat.

Since I suddenly had a lot of free time on my hands, I worked on my paper. I even made it to class on time.

However, if I ever wanted to sleep again, I needed to find out what Dad had done. I didn't know why I bothered coming to campus at all. I had no idea what any of my professors had said that day. Thoughts of paying off money that I didn't owe and certainly didn't have consumed my every thought. I didn't even remember how I got from one class to the next, or what I had for lunch. Wait, did I have lunch?

When we were finally released after my last session

for the day, I gratefully grabbed the notebook that only contained scribbles and the half-eaten breakfast bar I'd absentmindedly nibbled on and stuffed them in my bag. Before I had a chance to make a quick escape, a hand on my arm stopped me.

"Willa. What is going on with you today? Did you hear a word I just said?"

I turned to face an annoyed-looking Maisie. "Sorry, just got a lot on my mind. Try me again, and I promise I'll listen this time."

Maisie huffed out an exasperated breath. "Fine. I asked if you are still coming tonight."

She rolled her eyes at my blank look.

"Remy's party?"

Nope, didn't ring a bell. And the last thing I had time for was a party. She knew I hated those with a passion. Why she would insist I come along was a mystery to be solved another day.

"I can't. Have to go see my dad, and I was supposed to be working at the Donut Hole."

"I know you think you have some kind of responsibility to take care of him, but he's a grown man. He can take care of himself. It's time for you to realize that. Stop trying to save him."

The ever-present shame of my dad washed over me. I had been taking care of him for as long as I could remember.

The first memory I have of Dad is making him toast after Uncle Des brought him back from the police station. When I was nine, I had long taken over cooking us meals and doing the laundry. By the time I was fifteen, I had picked him up from Las Vegas because he had literally gambled all his money and possessions away, and hiding him from debt collectors was a regular occurrence.

I taught myself how to forge his signature to be able to pay our bills and lock him out of the account. That last one only lasted until he couldn't get money for his bar tab.

He was never violent. No matter how drunk or high he got, he would never lay a finger on me. He would make a mess and get too smashed to work, but he never once hurt me. He always had a kind word to say—except when I locked him out of his bank account. But when he wasn't drunk, things were great.

Unfortunately he was never sober for long, and every time he went on one of his binges, I wouldn't see him for days. Was it exhausting? Definitely. Did I have days I was ready to tell him to fuck off? Absolutely. But things were never black and white, and my dad hadn't always been this way. Or so I was told by Uncle Des.

I loved him fiercely, and I was protective, so anyone suggesting I should step back never sat well with me.

"You don't know what you're talking about. He needs me. And I'm going over there today instead of sitting at a pointless party, drinking warm beer while listening to some cocky jock droning on and on about the great passes he made at the game."

Maisie started to protest, but I cut her off. "I know that's the kind of party you're going to. You love football players. And don't deny it because all of the guys you've hooked up with since Ray have been big-headed, broad-shouldered, and on the team. I just can't go tonight. I'm sorry."

I knew I had won when Maisie tilted her head and puckered her lips expertly into an adorable pout. "Fine.

But don't think you'll get away that easily. I'm leaving in a few days."

She didn't need to remind me that I would be on my own for the summer. No chance I would ever forget. "And I'm going to spend time with you before you leave. Just not at another party. Now let me get out of here, or Dad will be too far gone to talk to me."

"All right, go on then and be the knight in shining armor once again. I hope he knows how epic you are."

I kissed her cheek before sprinting up the steps and out of the lecture hall. My bike was still were I had chained it to the bench outside. My car broke down again this morning, so I was back to riding my trusted bicycle. It was old, it was rusty, and more often than not, the chain came off. But until I had the money to replace my radiator, it would have to do.

The ride out to the trailer park my dad and uncle lived in was short, one of the advantages of living in a small town. One of the only advantages.

I waved at Mrs. Mandoon on my way through. Her dog Stevie in one hand and a cup of tea in the other, she looked fit to meet the queen. Always impeccably dressed, today was no exception. Not a white hair on her head was out of place, her pressed slacks and cream blouse spotless.

I regularly visited her for her world-famous muffins, a tradition that had started when she first moved in ten years ago after her husband made an epically bad investment in rubber ducks. He was now selling cars over on Fourth Street, but his income barely covered the rent for their trailer these days. Despite that, she always had cookies at the ready and a cup of tea filled whenever I came over.

I pulled up outside the old trailer that had seen

better days. Dad had sold the wheels years ago and propped it on blocks instead. He was not planning on moving it and always said he would stay there until the day he died. Uncle Des lived next door; his trailer wasn't looking much better, but at least it had all its wheels and windows that opened.

"Killa, hon, what are you doing here? Don't you have class?" Uncle Des called out from his position on the sofa he insisted had to stay outside year-round. According to him, outside was the only way to watch his big television.

"Stop calling me that. You know I hate it."

"You earned it fair and square. It was either you or the spider. Kill or be killed. And my little Killa came out victorious." Des smirked at me.

I was terrified of spiders but refused to kill them. Both my uncle and Dad were out during the fateful day I received my nickname and was forced to squash a spider. I was so upset over killing it that I cried and refused to leave my room for a few hours.

"Is Dad in?"

"He's taking a nap."

"Everything okay?"

Des avoided my gaze and stared with rapt attention at the gigantic flat-screen just inside his trailer. I bet tampon commercials were really interesting to him these days. He only moved inside when it rained, because according to him fresh air was as important as eating your daily greens.

"What happened?" I probed, pretty sure I already knew the answer.

"Nothing. Why would anything have happened? He was just tired. Can't a man be tired? Everyone likes a good nap. Nothing wrong with that."

"Des. How bad is it? Worse than last year?" I didn't need an answer. His refusal to look at me said it all.

The door to my dad's trailer was gone, lying neglected on the grass. He must have forgotten his key again.

I made my way into the trailer, through the messy lounge, and into Dad's bedroom. Sure enough he was passed out on his bed, fully dressed with dried puke in his hair and on his clothes. Great, now I had to change the sheets again. He was getting worse, and nothing I said or did helped. I was out of ideas.

I carefully shook his shoulder and hoped it wouldn't cause him to spew again. I knew from experience even the slightest movement could set him off.

A long groan tore out of him, his big body slowly rolling over. I stepped back just in case, but it seemed that wasn't necessary today.

"Willa?" He blinked at me in confusion. "Aren't you supposed to be in class? What are you doing here?"

"It's Friday. I finish early on Fridays. Something you should know since I pinned my schedule to your fridge and come over to cook for you every week." Disappointment hit me like a freight train.

He forgot my birthdays most of the time, and I would be surprised if he knew how old I was. I was used to his indifference, but sometimes the armor that I'd managed to build around myself got chipped and it hurt more than I could handle. Today was one of those days.

He wasn't the only one who'd lost someone.

"Sorry I woke you. I gotta go, just remembered I was supposed to meet Maisie," I said, desperate for an excuse to leave.

Dad didn't reply. Instead, he just rolled over and

went back to sleep. Must have been a big bender if he didn't even say goodbye.

I ground my teeth, knowing I would forgive him like I did every time, but his dismissal hurt.

The trailer felt suffocating; the stale smell of food and dirty clothes overbearing. I left without cleaning any of the dishes piling up or doing the laundry that was scattered across the floor. It was a terrible mess, but for once I didn't care. As soon as I stepped outside, I inhaled deeply, the fresh air helping to clear the odor out of my nose.

"Killa, do you think I should wear the Hawaiian shirt or the pink one for my date tonight?" Uncle Des said, holding up the two shirts in question. I ignored him and picked up my bike. The urge to get as far away from this place as possible was all-consuming. "Darling, where are you going?"

If Dad couldn't tell me how the hell he lost twenty grand, Des sure could. "What do you know about the money Dad owes the Drakes?"

Des clutched the shirts tighter, not meeting my eyes. And I had my answer.

He lifted his gaze, his eyes wide, the shirts now cradled to his chest. "Little rose, he thought it was a sure bet. Chances of losing were small. If the driver hadn't lost control over his car at the last corner, your dad woulda made a lotta money.

Same excuse, different bet. I had nothing left to say to him and turned away from his pleading eyes. "I'll see you later, Des."

I jumped on my bike and pedaled as hard as I could, desperate to put distance between me and my family. I didn't notice the tears until my vision blurred. I refused to stop, the only thing on my mind was to get back to my apartment and hide. My life was tumbling out of control, and I had no idea how to get it back on track.

I somehow made it without crashing. I struggled with the front door of the apartment complex as usual. The bitch always got stuck at the halfway point and only opened further if you pushed with the strength of a thousand angry kittens. On a normal day, I could have fit through the gap, but with my bike I struggled.

I was still crying, the tears unstoppable and making me angry. I have never liked crying. I was sure the door was now mocking me, and I punched it hard, causing pain to shoot through my hand. "Fuck you, you fucking useless piece of decaying wood. If you don't want to draw your last breath, you better open." I kicked it, and now my toes were hurting too. "Fuck." And just for good measure, I added another one. "Fuck."

I was now wedged between the door and my bike with a throbbing hand and foot. The door, of course, hadn't moved an inch. The fucker never did.

"Feel better?" someone asked from behind me.

And I had to admit I actually did feel better. My tears had finally stopped falling, and the fog had lifted from my brain. I wasn't sure how much damage I had done to myself, but I was fairly certain that I wasn't strong enough to break any bones with my twiggy arms.

I turned around and jolted back, smashing into my bike when I saw who was there. The handlebar dug into my back, and I huffed out in pain. I did not expect to see him again so soon. I wasn't ready. And I certainly didn't magically come up with the money. "What the fuck are you doing here?"

"Shit, you all right?" Jameson asked and reached his hand out to me. I flinched back and he immediately dropped it.

"I'm fine." I turned around and wiggled the bike handle that was wedged between the door and wall. It didn't budge. And why would it if it could so easily make my humiliation complete. Demon bike.

I felt Jameson's heat at my back and tensed. "Here, let me." His arm came around my waist and he pulled me back. I was too stunned to protest and let him guide me back like a little clueless lamb.

He was touching me. His arm was around my body. His chest was pressed to my back. And just like that, I forgot how to breathe or talk.

He released me once I was outside and took up the position I was previously in. One shove against the door and it opened. Of course it did. Smug bastard door.

Jameson pushed the bike inside and stopped to wait for me. I looked at my feet, wondering why they weren't moving. Nope, not stuck to the floor and definitely still attached to my body. Another sneaky glance from under my lashes confirmed Jameson was still there.

My feet finally decided to do my bidding, and I followed him inside. He carried my bike up to my floor and waited patiently while I unlocked the door. He didn't wait for an invitation but instead walked past me, leaving the bike next to the door.

"I found a way for you to pay off your debt," he announced.

"It's not my debt! So you don't need to find a way for me to pay it off. Because I won't pay off what I don't owe."

"Are we back to that again?" Jameson stalked toward me, and I shrank back into the kitchen. I hit the counter and watched with big eyes as he stalked closer and reached inside his pocket. I hoped he didn't think of this as the way to pay him off. Because there was no way. No matter how hot he was. Or how much I liked his eyes. Or his arms. Or his chest. Hair. Okay, I guess you get the point. But I would never sell myself. I had more pride than that.

He pulled papers out of his pocket and handed them to me.

I eyed them suspiciously but took them anyway, too curious to find out what they said.

The top of the page read "work contract," and I couldn't have been more surprised. "Are you offering me a job?" I asked, dumbfounded.

"I am. You can work for me full time over the summer and make a dent in your dad's debt. Once classes start again, you can do a few hours a week."

I was too stunned to do more than stumble toward my couch and sink down into the soft cushion. I landed on something hard, and when I put my hand underneath my butt to get it out, I froze. The dildo Maisie had given me the other day, the very one I had carelessly flung on the couch after unpacking it, was now poking me in the butt. I discreetly pushed it further underneath me, all the while praying Jameson wouldn't notice.

He had taken a seat on the other side of the couch, watching me shuffle back and forth. "I checked your finances. You are in more trouble than I thought."

"You did what?"

He ignored my outraged shriek and continued, "You're broke."

A snort escaped before I could stop it. "Thanks, Sherlock. That's not exactly news to me."

"So how do you propose you pay me back?"

I threw up my hands and waved them around. Why? I'm not sure. Maybe because I was upset. Maybe because if I didn't move something I'd try and lunge at him and his stubbornness. Rock-bottom, meet Willa.

"As I told you before, I don't gamble. Therefore, I don't owe you any money. So why don't you leave me alone and get out of my apartment? I have things to do."

His mesmerizing eyes pierced me with their intensity, and I gulped the saliva accumulating in my mouth. Must. Not. Drool.

"We all know your dad isn't going to pay me back. That leaves you."

My mouth went dry, and I realized it was pointless to continue arguing with him. "Since you know how broke I am, what do you propose I'll do to pay you back? Eat fairy dust and shit gold? I already have a job and don't see how I can add another one."

His lips twitched, but he didn't let himself smile. I bet he had a gorgeous smile. His lips were nice and full, his teeth straight, and I thought I glimpsed a hint of a dimple earlier. He ignored my smart-ass comment and narrowed his eyes at me. "You can work your debt off until you find a way to pay me back."

There was simply no reasoning with this man, and the only way to get him out of my apartment was to agree. "Fine. I'll do it. I have one more week of classes. After that I'll be free to work for you during the day. Now can you go?"

He studied me a moment longer, and I wished the floor would open up and suck me in. Anything would be better than being judged by Jameson.

"I'll message you the details." He got up. "And, Willa, don't think I won't come after you if you don't show up. I'm not a nice guy."

"No kidding. And here I thought I finally met the

man of my dreams." Since I was already at the bottom, might as well bang my head against it a few times to make it worthwhile.

He studied me for a moment before he shook his head and left. I had no time to feel sorry for myself because I had to get ready for my shift at the Donut Hole, a second job that I had to take to be able to pay Dad's bills and that I hated with a passion.

3

My night at the Donut Hole was long and busy. Jack, the owner, showed up halfway through the night, and like the drill sergeant he was, he yelled at us the whole way through the rest of our shifts. Steffi and Lynn ground their teeth every time he strutted past and made sure to get away as fast as possible.

I wasn't so lucky or coordinated and half the time was left with a lecture. A few months ago, he decided we all had to wear roller skates for work. I mean, seriously, did he not realize how hard it was to hold your tray steady while walking on your own two feet? Add a few wheels and you were screwed, and not in the way you wanted to be.

But I needed the job, so I put on the contraptions and shut my mouth. Before that he had changed our uniforms to polka dot shorts and a white T-shirt. The shirts became see-through every time we spilled something on them. And since the roller skates made everything a challenge, I ended up with a see-through shirt after nearly every shift.

"Willa," Jack called out for the tenth time that night,

causing me to spin on my skates and nearly trip over Lynn. He didn't like to be kept waiting, and I didn't like to lose my job. So I cursed silently, apologized to Lynn, and put as much of a smile on my face as I could manage while thinking of ways to avoid this conversation.

"You called," I said and stopped almost gracefully in front of him without losing the contents of my tray.

"Table three complained their fries were too spicy."

I fought the urge to roll my eyes. What the hell did they expect when they ordered chili cheese fries?

"I'll make sure they get a new plate. On the house," I said between clenched teeth.

Jack hated giving anything out for free. If he could, he would charge for the condiments and the tap water. He tried once, but people stopped coming and he dropped the idea. Didn't mean he wouldn't try again.

"Next time make sure they actually want chili on their fries."

I couldn't help but defend myself when I knew I should have just nodded and kept the half-assed smile on my face instead. "They did order the chili cheese fries. If they didn't want chili, they could have gotten regular fries."

"Just do your job," Jack boomed, and I gritted my teeth before skating to the kitchen to let Hank know. He was a great cook and didn't deserve to be told a customer didn't like their food because he made it exactly the way it was supposed to be made.

I leaned my head through the window to the kitchen and called out, "Hey, big guy, table three didn't like the chili on their chili cheese fries. Can you make it cheese fries?"

"Bloody dimwits," he said and nodded his head. "Comin' right up, doll."

I shot him an apologetic smile and back out I went. The night didn't go much better after that. I managed to spill a full glass of lemonade on my shirt and didn't have time to get changed because we were swamped. I did the only thing I could do and motherfucking owned it.

There wasn't much that was worse than a giant yellow stain on a transparent white shirt.

Except getting a call from the police station.

We weren't supposed to have our phones on us while we were working, so I only checked it during breaks. But since I didn't have time to take a break, I didn't see the missed call until I finished my shift at eleven.

As soon as I spotted the number on my phone, I groaned. I had seen it more times than I cared to remember. And every time it flashed on my screen, it meant Dad was in trouble. Suck a duck, the last thing I wanted to do was go down to the station and bail him out again.

With a heavy heart and crusty shirt, I hit Call. They picked up on the second ring.

"Willa, about time you called us back." It was true, they knew my number. Could recite it back to you if you asked. Thanks, Dad, for making me well-known around the Humptulips Police Department.

"Tony. Didn't know you were back from camping."

"Got back yesterday. Too many flies out there."

I liked Tony. He was nice, never raised his voice and always tried to get Dad out of trouble. I couldn't stop the sigh that escaped. "What did he do this time?"

"Found him at O'Malleys trying to punch Mason Drake. Something about owing money?"

Damn, I wished I didn't know what he was talking

about. Mason was Jameson's younger brother, and if my dad owed one of them money, he owed both of them. The brothers had always been close, and since they opened their garage, you hardly ever talked about one without the other coming up. Mason liked to run illegal car races, but I wasn't sure how much Jameson was involved.

"I'll come and get him."

"Appreciate it. He should have sobered up some by now."

I jumped on my bike and pedaled the ten miles to the station. And here I thought my night couldn't get worse.

4

"DAD," I GROANED, NEARLY BUCKLING UNDER HIS weight. "You have to help me out here. I can't carry you by myself. Use your legs."

I took a taxi to get us home, because walking was out of the question. The taxi dropped us off outside the trailer. Dad fell asleep on the way and was now barely able to get out of the car, let alone walk. His eyes closed again, and I struggled to hold him up.

This wasn't going to work. I needed help and money to pay for the cab. Stepping away from him, I slowly let go of his waist and he slid to the ground. Not fazed at all with his new position, he curled up and started snoring. If only this was the first time he'd gone to sleep outside his trailer.

With a deep sigh, I stepped over his body and navigated my way past the plants and random pots Uncle Des kept in front of his trailer. I noticed a giant hedge that had been added to his collection, wondering what he planned on doing with it. It also looked like it had been chopped in places.

I knocked on his door as hard as I could in the hopes

I could wake him up. He was just as heavy a sleeper as Dad. "Des, open up. I need your help."

A light came on, and Des's unruly mop of brown curly hair appeared in the doorway. "Whadda ya doin' here, sweetheart? Shouldna you be in bed gettin' ya beauty sleep?" He was still half asleep and mumbled his words more than usual. I had to listen closely to understand what he was saying.

"I'd love to do just that, but Dad's passed out on his front lawn. Can you give me a hand to move him inside?" I moved back toward the snoring form on the ground. "And do you have thirty dollars I could borrow for the taxi?"

Des scratched his head in confusion. "I thought he wasna goin' out t'night. He promised."

"He promises a lot of things. But when have you ever actually seen him follow through? My tree house? Two planks aren't enough to make a tree house. My old sandbox he was supposed to get rid of? Still there. And don't get me started on the kitchen table. Three legs, the missing one has been replaced with books. And all he has to do is get some glue and put the missing leg back on."

"Rightio. Gotcha. Let's get him inside."

We silently made our way to the sleeping form on the lawn. Des paid the cab fare before joining me at Dad's side. "Garret, man, wake up. Ya sleepin' on the ground again."

As expected, there was no response from Dad. I had done this many times before, and there was only one way to wake him up when he was passed out. With a resigned sigh, I made my way over to the outside tap and filled one of the old buckets lying around the yard. Only when it was nearly spilling over was I satisfied. It was a sad truth that we'd need more than a few drops.

There was no time to waste if I wanted to get any sleep tonight, so once I was close enough I dumped the entire thing on Dad. He immediately shot up, spluttering. "What? Who? What did I miss?" he yelled, wiping the water out of his eyes.

We helped him up and managed to drag him inside his trailer. We didn't quite make it to the bedroom, but the couch would do just fine. At least he was inside. He slumped in on himself and was passed out again as soon as his butt hit the cushion.

I looked at his still form, tears forming in my eyes. I hated having to do this over and over again. Every time he promised it wouldn't happen again, I would get another call. The longest he had ever made it without an incident was three weeks. Three measly weeks.

Des knew how much Dad's behavior upset me and put his arm around my shoulders like he'd done many times before. I needed more than a one-armed hug and turned into him, holding on tight and sniffling into his shoulder.

"There, there, girlie. No need to cry. He'll be right's rain t'morrow." Des didn't do well with tears and awkwardly patted my back. After allowing myself a moment to wallow in self-pity, I straightened back up. No need to cry about things I had no control over. One last wipe of my face on his shirt and I was ready to face the world again.

"Thanks, Des. I better get going."

He walked me out to my bike that the cab driver had generously allowed me to take in the trunk of his car. It helped that I knew his mom. She used to be my fifth-grade science teacher.

Des put his hand on my shoulder and squeezed lightly. "Take care, doll. It's gonna be okay." Always with the positive attitude.

Instead of answering, I got back on my bike and pedaled home.

5

The last week of classes went by with excruciating slowness. I handed in my assignment that I finished just before the deadline, which brought my accomplishments for the week up to one. Work was hell after the dishwasher at Sweet Dreams gave out, and Rayna and I were stuck washing everything by hand. It took forever and made Rayna impossible to work with. She hated doing dishes, and three days in a row was her limit. The new dishwasher was supposed to be installed on Thursday, but they didn't get around to doing it until Saturday. I had to pull a double shift at the Donut Hole on Sunday and didn't get home until after midnight.

Monday didn't treat me any better when my traitorous alarm didn't wake me up. It might have had something to do with me forgetting to set it. Fact was, I slept in. And now I was running late for my first day working for Jameson. It also turned out it took me almost an hour to get to Drake's Garage on my bike, something I failed to include in my timing. I was a sweaty mess by the time I pulled up outside the huge converted warehouse.

The garage was gigantic. A big roller door covered one side; the other was taken up by what looked like an office. I dropped my bike behind a pile of tires and made my way to the door off to the side. The sign marking it as the office was hanging on an angle, barely legible and covered in dust. The urge to clean it and put it back in its proper place was strong. But the urge not to be later than I already was propelled me forward, and with a loud creak of the door—something I had to have a look at because there was no way I was enduring that screeching every time someone came in—I finally set foot inside the office. Thirty-five minutes late.

"You're late," a gruff voice greeted me.

"I know. I'm sorry. It took me longer to get here because my bike is a piece of shit and the chain kept popping out. But I'll work late so you won't even notice."

My monologue fell on deaf ears. Jameson was standing behind a desk, looking like he was ready to tape my mouth shut and leave me for dead in the tire graveyard outside. I gulped but forged on, forcing cheer into my voice. I could do this. As long as I ignored his biceps, which I could make out all too clearly at that moment. His T-shirt was tight, his arms crossed over his impressive chest. I also couldn't look him in the eyes because of earlier mention of loss of brain function. I didn't think eyes could be that bright.

His hotness was most likely nature's way of keeping him alive. I couldn't be the only one he did his best to piss off and who wanted to shorten his life. I was sure that's what 80 percent of the population would want to do if they spoke to him for more than five minutes. The other twenty just wanted to jump his bones. No talking necessary. Scratch that. Make it fifty-fifty.

"Where do you want me to start?" The cheer was still in my voice as I studied the filing cabinet a little too intently. It was sitting in the middle of the room, and I had to walk around it if I wanted to get to the desk. Weird setup.

"Answer the phones. If anyone comes in, you come and get me." The back door slammed shut and he was gone. Introduction over.

I studied the dusty office and developed asthma from just looking at it. Calling it filthy would be a compliment. It was a dump. And there was no way I would be spending the next few months working in conditions detrimental to my health.

I dropped my bag on the desk, or rather on the papers covering the desk, and got to work. After I opened a few random doors—note to self, if it says male toilet it probably is—I found a mop.

The cleaner was stashed under the sink in the small staff kitchen that would also require a thorough cleaning, but I would get to that next. The phone was ringing when I made my way back to the office. I was breathless from my sprint to get to it on time and was hardly able to get out a "Drake's Garage, how may I help you?"

"You the new girl?"

"Yes, sir."

"Started today?"

"Correct, sir."

"You know anything about a job for Stamos?"

"If you give me a minute, I'll look it up in the system."

The guy on the line laughed long and hard. Not sure what was so funny about my offer to help him out.

"J hasn't filed shit in years. The only one who knows

anything about the job is J. Just tell him to call Ron. He'll know what it's about."

"No problem. Will do."

"Try to last longer than a week. The last receptionist cost me a lot of money when she left after three days. I'm gonna bet two weeks this time. Don't quit before then."

"I'll give it my best shot. Have a good day."

We hung up and I sank back into the office chair. It was soft and comfortable, and I didn't want to get back up. When my gaze fell on the grimy floor, I decided cleaning this shithole was a life-or-death situation. In between answering more phone calls, I managed to scrub the room from top to bottom.

I even washed the two large windows facing the front of the office. The door at the back led to the garage, and the only other door was connected to a hallway that led to the kitchen and toilets.

I moved the desk into a corner, which opened up the space. The couch, two armchairs, and coffee table now sat in front of one of the windows in the opposite corner to my desk. I attempted to move the large filing cabinet, but it was huge and wouldn't budge an inch. Moving all the other furniture was a feat in itself, but I was determined, and bored.

The filing cabinet, on the other hand, could wait because no matter how hard I pushed, it just wasn't happening.

I turned to sorting out the mountain of papers on the desk instead. It would take me days to get through them, but at least I was able to get enough filed away to uncover the computer. It looked brand new, and I clapped my hands in delight when it turned on. I quickly realized why the computer looked spotless.

There were no files on it, no trace of anyone actually using it. It was brand new.

"The hell?" a voice came from the door. "How did you clean all this up so quickly?"

I turned and was met with a curious stare. The guy was around my age, had curly dark brown hair and green eyes. He smiled at me, and I stared at an adorable dimple. I gave him my best *"I'm nice, so be my friend"* smile and held out my hand.

"I'm Willa, your new receptionist."

He shook my hand, his grip firm. "Landon. I hope you know what you're doing." He released me and turned in a semicircle, taking in the now clean office and murmured, "I knew I should have taken the one-day bet."

"Can you give me a hand?" I asked, ignoring his comment and pointing to the gigantic cabinet that was sitting in the middle of the room. "I want to push this against the back wall, but it's too heavy."

"That thing weighs a ton. I'll get Clayton to give me a hand." He opened the back door and yelled, "Clay. Get your ass into the office. You gotta see this."

Another guy came through the door. He was so tall and wide he had to duck to enter, his big body immediately commandeering the space. "That the new girl?"

"In the flesh," I responded, my big smile still firmly in place. "I'm Willa." I held my hand out again in greeting. He took it, and I winced at his hard grip.

"Clay." He scratched his head and stared at the desk, shaking his head. "Shoulda said one day. Damn it."

I ignored his comment just as I had ignored Landon's. These guys were a little strange.

"Give me a hand with the cabinet. Willa wants it pushed against the wall," Landon said.

Clay shook his head but helped him anyway. "Forget a day. I'll give her another hour. At most," Clay said to nobody in particular.

I turned in a circle, happy about the new look of the office. It was now clean, spacious, and gave off all the best zen. With a big grin on my face, I thanked the guys, who were watching me curiously. "You are the best. Thank you so much." And because I couldn't help myself, I clapped my hands.

"Great to have you on board," Clay said on his way out, and Landon winked at me.

Maybe working here wouldn't be as bad as I thought. At least they seemed nice.

I spent the next hour answering more pointless calls. Everyone just wanted to speak to Jameson or one of the guys since I didn't know squat about any of the jobs they asked about. My call list was taking up two pages, and I debated whether or not I should go and find Jameson.

I was still unable to make up my mind if it was a better idea to clean the grimy kitchen instead of facing the Neanderthal when the back door opened again. I turned my chair. The new position of the desk was perfect for seeing all angles in the office. I did a great job with the redesign, if I did say so myself.

Jameson, who had come inside, apparently didn't think so. His face was red as his eyes darted around the office. I expected him to have a fit any minute now. It took about two point five seconds for him to lose his shit.

"What. The. Fuck. Have. You. Done?" Each word was clipped short.

Undeterred by his foul mood, I put my best nonthreatening smile on my face and pushed down the urge to throw the computer screen at him. "I maximized your space and cleaned all the mold off your wall and floors. The dust is gone too; you don't want your customers to suffocate to death. That's a lawsuit waiting to happen."

"They hardly ever come in here, so that's never been an issue before," he thundered. "I told you to answer the phones. Nothing else."

"You didn't exactly imply I wasn't allowed to do anything else. You just said watch the phones. That doesn't mean I can't do a little cleaning. Or filing. When was the last time you opened that filing cabinet? And do you mind if I file everything by last name?"

I remembered the list on my desk and picked it up. "Before I forget, this is the list of calls you need to answer."

He took the piece of paper out of my hand and without another word stomped out, slamming the door behind him. Unbelievable. I was doing him a favor. We all knew how quickly people sued these days.

Deciding not to dwell on his ungrateful ass, I went about cleaning the kitchen. It didn't take as long as the office and was less disgusting than expected. The phone only rang a few times during the afternoon, and by the time I was done for the day, my back was aching and I was ready to go home.

Since I didn't know how long I was supposed to work, I went into the garage to find Jameson.

Landon was working in the bay closest to the door, and I walked over.

"Hey, Landon, do you know where Jameson is?"

"He left."

"He left? But he can't just leave. I still have messages for him. And I don't know how long I'm supposed to work for. Does that mean I can just go home?" *Please let it mean I can get home and forget I ever started working at Drake's.*

"The office usually stays open till five. You can keep working after that to do the filing and other shit, but you only need to answer the phones until then. Seeing as it's seven already, you should go home. He won't be back today."

"Motherfucker." It just came out. I had no control over my mouth.

Landon heard me and laughed. "I think you'll fit in just fine. You might even last for a little while. The record currently stands at eight days. Think you can beat that?"

That sounded like a challenge to me. "You can bet your perfect ass that I can beat that." Little did they know I also didn't have much of a choice. It was either working here or owing Jameson a lot of money.

I waved at Landon and Clay, grabbed my bag out of the office, and got on my bike to start my long trek home. I made it in an hour and fell into my bed, fully clothed. I didn't even bother to take my shoes off.

6

I HATED PASTRY SHEETS. I REALLY DID. THEY WERE slippery little fuckers. I never got them shaped right, and in the end, everything fell apart. My frustration levels were at an all-time high, and I had consumed four cups of coffee in the last two hours. Don't judge, it was an emergency. I normally stopped at three cups; the fourth always seemed to push me over the edge.

Today was no exception. I was unable to stand still, and my hands were shaky. *I should eat something. Or maybe drink a glass of water. Oooooh, delicious cupcakes. Aunt Rayna won't notice if I just ate one.*

Of course I was caught in the act, the cupcake half eaten when Rayna came back from her morning errands. She took one look at me and grinned. "Too much coffee?"

I nodded and stuffed the rest of the amazing cupcake in my mouth.

"I'll make you a sandwich. But only if you clean up your mess." She pointed to the bench I usually worked on and pulled out a loaf of bread. If Rayna offered to make you a sandwich, you did whatever she requested.

She was not only an amazing baker but a kick-ass cook and sandwich maker. The lady was gifted. She was also my favorite—and only—aunt. She was my rock when Dad was at his lowest and the person who held me together when Mom died.

Rayna was mom's sister. The two were as close as sisters could get, despite their twenty-year age gap. I called her Aunt Rayna only when I wanted to piss her off, since she was only five years older than me. She was the surprise baby. My grandparents—her parents—died when she was twelve, and she moved in with us.

I took a look at the pastry massacre and swallowed the last of my cupcake. There wouldn't be any croissants or pizza tarts on today's menu. I had thoroughly messed them all up.

After I scrubbed the bench clean, I happily accepted my sandwich. It smelled delicious. My fingers were only a little twitchy, and I was almost able to stand still again.

"Thanks, Rayna, you're a lifesaver."

"Now let me show you how to work with puff pastry since you seem to have forgotten."

She grabbed new sheets from the tray and started rolling them out. After a few practiced flicks of her hand, she had a perfectly shaped croissant laid out in front of her. She made it look so easy.

"Go already, I know you'll be no use to me after that much caffeine. I'll be monitoring your intake next time, young lady. I'm paying you to bake, not to make a mess."

"Promise it won't happen again. At least not this week."

I kissed her cheek and flew out the door, my legs grateful to be moving in a direction instead of jumping in the same place.

I arrived at Drake's Garage fifteen minutes early, a fact I loudly pointed out when I walked into the office. The very empty office with nobody around to share my moment of greatness.

I got busy making myself another cup of instant coffee—which was the brew of the misguided if you asked me—and started filing the huge pile of papers that were still on the desk.

Landon came in a little after twelve. "Willa, you came back." He was grinning at me, his dimple showing. "And you managed to get through some of the filing. Impressive."

I was so grateful for the distraction, I jumped up from my desk when I saw him and hugged him. He smelled of oil and soap, something I could get used to. His body was vibrating from the silent chuckles he was trying to hold back. He patted my back. "It can't be that bad."

I was about to tell him that there was nothing worse than the nonexistent filing system that Jameson had going on when the door opened again.

"Landon," Jameson ground out, looking none too happy as usual. "Don't you have work to do?"

"Just helping Willa get settled, boss man." Landon the coward stepped back, and with a nod to Jameson and a wink at me, he left me alone with the Neanderthal.

"Stay away from my staff. I don't need any drama at work," Jameson said.

"Excuse me? What exactly are you implying?"

"I meant exactly what I said. Stay away from the guys."

I was fuming mad, and he knew it since he took a step back after he saw my face. "I wasn't coming on to anyone, you jerk. I was just glad someone took pity on me and checked that I hadn't been smothered by all the paperwork yet."

I wasn't proud to admit this, but my voice was raised to an unprofessional level. The caffeine was still cruising through my veins, and I had been up since three in the morning after a restless night. "And I can hug whomever I want." Take that, jackass.

Said jackass crossed his arms over his chest and scowled at me. "Well don't. It's unprofessional, and we don't hug in this office. So I would appreciate it if you would refrain from doing so."

"And what if I don't?"

"You will stop hugging people in this office."

Oh, but I so wasn't done. "What are you gonna do? Fire me? How am I going to pay off the debt I owe you? We both know I don't have the money."

"Stop arguing. It's a simple request. One that you should be able to follow."

I was irrational. I knew this. I also knew that I should back down. It was a little inappropriate to hug people in the office, but I was a hugger. Every time I was upset, I hugged someone. Every time I was happy, I hugged someone. It was just the way I worked. And because I wasn't ready to just let this go, I did what I did best. I screwed things up further.

I brushed past him and into the garage and went up to Landon who greeted me with a big smile. "Hey, little lady, what can I do for you?"

I walked right up to him and hugged him. He was surprised at first, but after his initial confusion, he put his big paws around me and hugged me back.

I could feel Jameson behind me, and his presence was confirmed when I heard a loud "Fuck this shit."

I walked up to Clay who was eyeing me warily and hugged him, too. He awkwardly patted my back, clearly uncomfortable with a hug from a near stranger.

The last person that was working at the garage was Jameson's brother Mason. I had met him before, and he looked like a younger version of Jameson. We were in the same year at school, and he was always nice to me. When he saw me approach, he held out his arms, grinning wide. "If it isn't Willa Montgomery pissing off my brother."

I stepped into his outstretched arms, and he lifted me off my feet and spun me around. "Hey, Mason, how have you been?"

"What's with the hugging?" he asked, amusement laced in his voice.

I looked over my shoulder at Jameson who was watching us with narrowed eyes. *Take that, you jackass.*

Mason shook his head at me. "He tell you hugging was inappropriate behavior in the workplace or some shit like that?"

"That's exactly what he told me. So we are going to hug every day." I was mighty proud of myself for thinking of that little gem.

"Don't poke the bear, Willa." Mason ruffled my hair. "But it sure will bring some life into this place."

"You done with the Impala yet? They need it by this afternoon," Jameson said, his voice barely more than a growl.

Mason shot me an apologetic glance. "Duty calls. I'll try and drop in later so we can catch up."

He turned back to the car he was working on, and I skipped back to the office. And my victory skip was even better when I felt Jameson's eyes burning into my back the entire way.

I was still on a high when I made the decision to order a coffee machine. There was no way I could continue drinking that vile instant poison. I had two cups, and now I felt ill. Could also be due to the pizza I ate for lunch. The guys all dropped in to eat with me, something that was as unexpected as it was welcome. Jameson stayed away, but that wasn't a surprise.

Clay bought the pizza because apparently he lost a bet. And since I was the reason he lost, the guys insisted they had to share their winnings with me.

"So, Willa, what do you do when you're not trapped in this factory of awesomeness?" Clay asked me. His mohawk was spiked up today, and I loved it. I had to resist the urge to touch it. Despite the hugging, we were definitely not at the random hair-touching stage yet.

"I work at Sweet Dreams in the mornings and the Donut Hole at night. I also go to Winchester. Doesn't leave much time for anything else."

I looked up from my pizza and found them all staring at me. I shifted on my seat, uncomfortable with the sudden attention and not sure what I said wrong.

"You work three jobs?" Landon asked, blinking his big eyes at me.

"Two and a half. I'm at Sweet Dreams five days a week and the Donut Hole three nights. Sometimes more if they need me to help out."

"That's a lot of hours. I thought you were studying," Clay said.

I shrugged. "I am studying. But I also have to pay the bills. I wasn't planning on getting another job, though."

Landon shook his head. "So why would you spend your summer, the only time you get to actually do what you want, working at this place? Don't get me wrong, we desperately need a receptionist, but why would you agree to do it? Surely you can't be that hard up for cash."

"It's complicated." And there wasn't a choice on whether or not I'd be working here. I got up and started cleaning the desk that was covered in pizza boxes. I was glad nobody asked more questions. After a scuffle on who got the last piece, they went back to the cars they were working on, and I was left with my paperwork. Goody.

I continued taking messages and cleaning the desk. After a few hours, I was so bored I would welcome any distraction, even if it came in the form of Jameson, which led me to the fateful decision to look up coffee machines online. I also got a hold of Mason's credit card. He had handed it to me earlier, just in case I needed to order anything for the office.

The wall clock that now had brand-new batteries and was once again hanging up, thanks to yours truly, told me that it was already past six. I hadn't seen Jameson since the hugging incident. I couldn't really blame him. It was childish on my part, but I just continuously seemed to be losing my shit whenever he opened his mouth to yell at me. I left his messages on the desk, easy for him to find now that I'd filed away all the papers and gathered my things that I had spread all over the office.

I checked my phone for the first time today and saw that I had three missed calls from Uncle Des. He usually just left a message when I didn't answer. My stomach tied itself in knots while I made up possible worst-case scenarios in my head. I just hoped Dad hadn't borrowed a police car again. I didn't think we could get him out of a charge this time.

Des picked up after the first ring. "Willa. Been tryna reach you all day, girl."

"I was at work and just saw your missed calls. Is everything all right?"

"Tony called me."

I groaned loudly, knowing where this was going. "Not again. Twice in one week? Really?"

"I would have picked him up, but I'm in Florida at that conference. Can you go get him?"

"Fine. Do I need to bail him out?"

"I put money in your account. Use it. I didn't know you'd been paying his bail. You shoulda told me."

The last thing I wanted to do was burden someone else with my problems, and bailing Dad out of jail was nobody else's problem but mine. "It was nice of you to do that but not necessary."

"Honey, ya gotta accept help every once in a while. Now stop bein' so stubborn and take it, 'cause I don't want it back."

I knew I hit a brick wall when Des started handing out life advice. "Fine. I'll use it." I also didn't have a choice since I was broke and had used my car as leverage last time I had to bail Dad out.

"Thanks, Killa. I'll see you in two days. Oh, and if ya see one of the Martins, tell 'em their hedge is coming. I didn't think things through when I drove to that nursery place on my scooter. The hedge wouldn't fit, and they have to deliver it."

We said our goodbyes and hung up. I was not looking forward to riding my bike out to the police station. It was over twenty miles.

Landon was coming out of the workshop as I was pulling out my bike from behind the tires. Uncle Des's words still fresh in my mind, I decided this was a good time to swallow my misplaced pride and ask for help. "Hey, Landon, are you going up near Cook's by any chance?"

"Sorry, Willa, I'm headed toward the lake. Live out there."

"Okay, no problem. See you tomorrow."

"I hope you're not planning on riding your bike all that way. It's a long way, and half of that is freeway."

"I don't think I have much of a choice seeing as there's something wrong with my car."

Landon came closer and raised his brows at me. "You do remember that you work at a garage, right? We fix cars here."

"Huh, now that you mention it, I was wondering what all that noise out the back was."

He tugged a strand of my hair and shook his head. "Bring it in tomorrow, and I'll have a look at it."

"Can't. It's not starting."

Landon took his phone out of his pocket and held it out to me. "Put in your number and address, and I'll get it towed."

I didn't waste any time doing as I was told, eager to get going since it would take me ages to get to the police station.

"Jameson is going over to Butler to get parts he ordered. He can drop you off on the way."

"Oh no, that's okay, I'll just—"

"Yo, J, you still going to pick up those parts?"

Jameson came out of the garage and walked toward us. He had oil on his cheek, and I itched to swipe it off. "Sure am. Why? You need something from Butler?"

"Willa here needs a lift to Cook's. Can you drop her off on the way?"

Jameson fixed me with his beautiful eyes. Eyes that

were wasted on a jackass like him. Even his lashes were long and full, every girl's dream. And don't get me started on his hair. I had an unhealthy relationship with it. It was dark and full and so shiny; I just wanted to sink my hands into it. Oh, the fun me and that hair could have. If only it wasn't attached to jerkface. And of course there was the hair-touching issue again. Definitely too early for moves like that.

"Okay. I'm leaving in five," he said, face expressionless as usual.

I didn't get a chance to respond to either one of them since Jameson walked back inside the garage and Landon jumped in his car. After a wave in my direction, he took off with squealing tires.

I stood next to my bike, not sure if I should be excited that I was about to be stuck with Jameson or scared out of my white cotton panties with pink elephants. As soon as Jameson came back out and walked to his truck, not sparing me one glance, I decided to go with option number two.

My bike was so old, the heavy frame wasn't just a pain to ride on, it was also too heavy for me to lift. But that's exactly what I would have to do to get the demon mobile on the bed of Jameson's truck.

I stopped in front of the back tailgate and opened it. Step one complete. I then proceeded to lift the front end high enough to rest on the edge of the open tailgate. I was huffing at that stage, cursing the fact that I never lifted weights. Or went to the gym.

Before I could execute the next step, two big arms appeared in my vision. "I've got it," Jameson's gruff voice told me, and I stepped back. I wasn't going to be stubborn and demand to do it myself. Because I knew without a doubt I wouldn't be able to. Before he offered his help, I had been close to becoming a headline in the papers. *Beautiful life cut short by demon bike.*

"Thanks," I said, watching him lift the demon machine onto the back of his truck without so much as taking a deep breath. One lift of his big bulky arms, and it was done.

We got in the truck, and that's when things got awkward.

But really, what did I expect? He liked to talk in grunts and didn't know the meaning of the word "manners." I did my best to ignore smelling his damn soap that lingered on his skin. And that was even after a day of working at the garage. I really did try.

But a girl was only so strong when in close proximity to Jameson. Many had tried to resist and failed. I knew this because back in high school there was a Facebook page dedicated to him. People—or, more accurately, women—posted on there all the time. It was ridiculous. Not that I looked at it often. Only to find out what all the hype was about, and then again to find out how many likes he had. Three thousand if you were wondering. And the last time was just to show the site to Maisie and Stella, who were equally as appalled as I was.

He had left high school over five years ago, so I was sure someone had taken the page down by now. Maybe I should check to make sure. I'd be doing him a favor, really, looking out for him like that. I was such a Good Samaritan.

I decided to break the awkward silence with something friendly. We had to get over our animosity sometime. "Thanks for giving me a ride. You didn't have to."

"Going that way anyway."

His gruff answer was delivered in his typical dismissive fashion. Fine, I wanted to sit in silence and stare out the window anyway.

I didn't say anything else but give him directions. "Take the next exit."

He turned, and we were off the freeway. The road noise quieted to a hum when we slowed down, and I directed him to the police station. When he stopped out front, he looked at me with a questioning brow.

I avoided his gaze and opened the door. "Don't ask."

He got out on his side and took my bike down. I held on to the handle tightly and made my way toward the front entrance. "Thanks for the ride."

I looked back and saw him standing next to his truck, arms crossed over his chest, watching me. I felt a shiver go over my traitorous body when I watched him.

I had never been an overly sexual person, never felt the need to jump on someone or risk combusting. And he hadn't even done anything yet. I really needed to get the name of the therapist Stella was seeing. Things were getting out of control.

I left my bike outside, leaning it against the wall, and made my way inside. "Hey, Lucy, how are things? How's the pie business?" I asked the receptionist.

"Willa, if it isn't my favorite little baking queen. You'll be glad to hear that I did Humptulips proud last weekend and won the red pie baking competition. I used the strawberry recipe you helped me work on. It went down a treat."

I was giddy with excitement at her win. We had been working on her recipe for weeks. I rushed around the counter, something that was usually forbidden unless you wanted to get arrested. But seeing as I was here damn near every week, I got special privileges. And we shared a common love for hugs.

"Congratulations, I knew you could do it," I said and threw my arms around her.

"Thanks, Willa, couldn't have done it without you."

She sat back down at her desk, and I waved her off. "Don't be silly. Of course you could have. Your pies kick ass. No better ones out there."

She blushed at my compliment, and I knew I had said the right thing.

"Willa. You here for your old man?" a voice interrupted us.

"Tony. I sure am. What'd he do this time?"

"Took the Lancaster's satellite dish down."

I dropped my head in defeat. This wasn't the first time Dad had been arrested for dismantling his neighbor's satellite dish. He insisted it was obstructing his view. Of what, I wasn't so sure. There were only trailers and a dump out there.

"Did they press charges this time?"

"I managed to talk them out of it, but only if he puts it all back exactly the way it was. Sorry, Willa, might have to get someone out to get it done."

I gulped at the thought of having to pay for someone to come out. My budget was already stretched, and there was no way I could pay someone without having to eat ramen noodles for the next year. I hated ramen noodles.

"I'll make sure it gets done. Sorry to make you drive all the way out there again."

"No problem, hun. I'll get him so you can take him home. Try and stop him from doin' it again though, yeah?"

"Of course."

He went to get Dad while I completed the paperwork with Lucy. She shot me a pitying look that I hated but sadly was all too used to.

Tony brought Dad out, but I didn't look at him. He knew I was upset. One look at my face told him everything. I had never been good at hiding my emotions.

He followed me out of the station without a word. When I got my bike and turned toward the street only to see a familiar truck, I nearly rolled over my bike in my haste to get away.

Jameson was leaning against the door, arms crossed, watching me intently. Another shiver went down my body, and I jumped at the sensation. He needed to stop looking at me.

I tried to walk past him, but the fact that he had clearly waited for me to come back out should have told me I wouldn't get away without talking to him.

"Mr. Montgomery. Good to see you again," Jameson said.

He was entirely too civil. This was the man who owed him a shitload of money. Someone he watched walk out of jail after committing yet another crime. And he greeted him like they were old bowling buddies.

"I'll give you a lift home. Or if you want me to drop you off somewhere along the way, I'd be happy to," he said.

"Jameson, good to see you again. Home is just fine for now. I gotta go and see if my neighbors have put their satellite dish up again. That thing is a monstrosity. Nobody needs a thousand channels in their life. Nobody."

"Dad," I drew the word out to let him know I meant business. "Part of your release agreement is that you put the dish back up. Don't even think about doing anything else."

"I have a right to a view. And that impossible dish is destroying it. I'm not putting it back up."

Not willing to continue the argument in front of Jameson, who was paying us entirely too much attention, I pushed my bike toward the road. "Let's discuss it at home." I turned to Jameson. "Thanks for the offer, but if you drop us off, you'll be late to pick up your parts. They close in thirty minutes. I'll see you tomorrow."

Jameson ignored me and instead lifted my bike and placed it in the back of his truck. My protest was weak, and I only managed a grumbled "Hey" before he opened the passenger door and motioned us inside. "Hop in."

Too stunned to protest, I watched Dad get into the passenger seat. With no other option except to take the bus, I climbed into the back.

I realized the error of my choice immediately when Dad started talking about his homemade schnapps. He loved making the vile poison and could chew your ear off about the best way to make the stuff. To my surprise, Jameson responded when necessary and asked questions as if he was actually interested.

I just didn't understand him. Part of me didn't want him to get along with Dad. I most definitely didn't want him to see where I grew up. And where I would most likely be living again soon unless Dad stopped making me pay for his bail.

We pulled up to the trailer, and I cringed at the chaos. The yard was a mess, and I spotted empty bottles and food wrappers littering the ground. Jameson parked and got out. He put my bike up against the garden bench and turned back to Dad.

"Do you have the tools you used to get the dish down?"

Dad pointed to where the dish lay on the ground, tools scattered all around it. "They're over there. I didn't get a chance to put them away before they arrested me."

I watched in confusion as Jameson picked up the ladder, put it on the side of the neighbor's trailer, and climbed up, tools and half the dish in hand. After fastening the base, he came back down to get the rest. I stepped in front of him before he got far. "What do you think you're doing?"

"I thought that was obvious." He tapped the dish he was holding and walked around me.

"Okay, then why are you doing it?"

"You need the dish back up. I'm putting it back up."

I didn't really have an answer for him this time. Because I did need the dish back up, and I didn't have the money to pay for it. His kindness was surprising. I was grateful for his help because there was no way I could do it myself.

With that thought, I shut up—something that was as frustrating as it was exhausting—and took a step back to get out of his way. I should accept his help with grace and move on. It would be the right thing to do, but it was hard. Especially when the help came from Jameson.

He finished putting everything back up in no time at all. "Where do you want the tools?" He asked Dad who pointed to the table. "Leave 'em there. Willa's gonna put them away later."

I ground my teeth at his statement. I knew I would be the one to clean up the mess, but it still didn't feel good to have Dad point it out. He made me look like his maid.

"Where do they go?" Jameson asked me.

I shook my head. "It's all right. I have to clean up anyway."

"Willa." His tone suggested I should stop arguing.

My brain, on the other hand, suggested I should continue arguing. "It's fine. Really. I've got it."

He shook his head but did as instructed. I bet he couldn't wait to get out of here. Which he did, thankfully. He lightly put a hand on my arm, and I nearly didn't hear him when he said, "I'll see you tomorrow."

His touch lingered long after he'd gone, and I realized just how much trouble I was in. I was the moth drawn to the flame, and I would get burned if I got too close.

I ended up staying at Dad's until nearly midnight.

"I'm going to water the grass," Dad declared and heaved himself out of his chair. I stood up to block his path.

"Sit back down." I stood in front of the door to prevent him from going outside.

"Nothing wrong with wanting to take care of my lawn," Dad grunted but backed away from the door.

It was late. I was tired. And sick of babysitting Dad. "Can you act like a responsible adult for once in your life and promise me to leave the dish alone?"

Dad scratched at the leather of his worn chair, a task that required all his attention.

I tried again. "Dad, please. If I want to have any hope of being a functioning human tomorrow, I need to get some sleep, but I won't go home until you promise."

"Fine."

"Say it."

He grimaced but looked at me this time. "I promise not to try and take the ugly monstrosity down tonight."

Des would be back in the morning. If I could keep

Dad from doing anything stupid until then, we'd be good.

"I'll see you tomorrow." I hugged Dad and stepped out of the trailer. The cold wind hit me like a brick, and I sucked in a sharp breath. Big mistake, because now my lungs were frozen solid. I coughed and cackled until my body got used to being flash frozen. The ride home was going to be fun. I was only in my T-shirt, not anticipating being outside until late.

I wished I had my old ratty jacket. Maisie called it an eyesore, and Stella said it made me look homeless. I thought it was warm and comfortable.

As predicted, I was frozen solid by the time I got home, my hands and fingers numb. I fought with the front door, eventually pushing it open enough to get through. I dragged myself up the stairs, barely managing to pull my bike up behind me. I was sure I made more noise than necessary but just didn't care. I felt like shit and was ready to drop into bed.

And that's exactly what I did as soon as I put the bike inside the apartment where it landed with a loud bang. I just hoped I wouldn't sleep through my alarm again.

7

I SLEPT THROUGH MY ALARM AGAIN. WHEN I FINALLY made it to Sweet Dreams, Rayna had already finished a whole batch of cookies that looked like… penises?

I must have said it out loud because she harrumphed and shot me an evil glare. "Those are Christmas decorations." She pointed at the penis. "Candle." And moved on to the balls. "Baubles."

"Right. Looks great. Especially since it's October and all." I tied my apron and washed my hands, something that was as routine to me as breathing. "Where do you want me?"

"I'm practicing for Christmas, and you're late."

"I know. I'm sorry."

"Punctuality is the politeness of kings."

Someone had studied her inspirational quotes last night.

I spotted the list of orders for today and picked the top one. Cherry pie. Something I could bake in my sleep. Which I might have to since my eyes were still only half open. Where was the coffee?

By the time we finished all the orders, my head was throbbing and I was barely able to stand up straight.

"You look a little green, dear," Rayna not very helpfully pointed out.

"Didn't get enough sleep," I responded in between sips of coffee. I didn't go as crazy as yesterday, but I doubted I would have felt the effects anyway. I was dead on my feet. And my day had only just started.

"Get out of here. We're all finished, and I can manage putting everything out into the shop by myself."

"You sure?"

"Opportunity comes but does not linger."

Oh, kill me now. "Needed some inspiration yesterday?"

"You know it. There wasn't anything on television, so I decided to catch up on my reading."

I certainly didn't linger and wait for more quotes. Instead I made my way over to Drake's Garage. Maybe I could sleep a little before anyone came into the office.

The door was unlocked when I got there. A look at the time confirmed the phones wouldn't start ringing for an hour. Grateful for the short reprieve, I dropped onto the couch. It was comfortable and long enough that I could just lie down. I would just rest my eyes for a minute before I got started.

"We should wake her up."

"But she looks so peaceful."

"Like a princess."

"More like a child. Look how small she is."

"But we need her to talk to the delivery guy. I'm not signing for the coffee machine."

"Neither am I."

"Not it."

The voices sounded familiar. I slowly opened my eyes and looked at three curious faces. I stretched my tired limbs, still feeling exhausted.

"How long have you been staring at me?" I asked and heaved my body into a seated position.

"Not too long."

"Ten minutes."

"Just got here."

They all answered at the same time. I guess it was safe to say they had been here long enough to push them into the creep territory. I was too tired to care and waved them off.

"What time is it?"

"Almost nine."

Shit. I got up and made my way past Landon, Mason, and Clay.

"There's a delivery you need to sign for," Landon said and pushed a pad into my hand.

I took it and scribbled my name at the bottom. Satisfied, he went outside, where I could see him speak to a delivery guy. They talked for a few minutes before going to the back of the van and coming out with a giant coffee machine.

Huh, I knew I had ordered one but didn't think it was that big. Looked smaller in the photo.

They carried it inside, the giant machine almost as wide as the door.

"Jameson's gonna flip his shit," Clay said on his way to the back door, the glee evident on his face.

Landon came back out of the kitchen where they put the coffee machine and grinned at me. "I take my coffee black with two sugars."

"Coming right up," I said and went to test out the glorious machine. I really did have great ideas sometimes.

8

It was official. I was in love. I had never tasted better coffee. Not even Rayna was able to make coffee more glorious than what I was currently holding in my hand. I made all the guys a cup and was pretty happy with my fantastic idea to buy the machine. I also managed to file every single piece of paper that was still on my desk and now had a great system in place: sorting papers alphabetically.

Who would have thought something so simple could mean I'd be able to find anything in the span of a few seconds. I was mightily happy with myself.

I was tired, but my spirits were high and I thought I had finally worked out this job. I still wasn't able to answer any enquiries unless they included opening hours for the shop. Every time someone wanted to book in a job, I had to ask one of the guys when they were free, which brought me to my next genius project. I needed to make a schedule for everyone to keep track of their jobs. *That* could wait until after I had my delicious cup of heaven.

The loud bang of the door caused me to spill coffee

all over the floor. Jameson came stalking in, not acknowledging me but going straight to the door that led into the kitchen. The next thing I heard was a loud growl. He sounded like a wolf. A very unhappy wolf.

"Willa," he yelled. My eyes went wide, my hands started trembling, and I broke out in a cold sweat. That was definitely not a nice, "come and have a chat with me" call. It was an "if you're not in here in two seconds, I'll burn all your dolls and hang their carcasses off my car" yell.

I clutched my mug and tiptoed into the kitchen. Jameson was standing in front of the coffee machine, arms crossed as he seemed to like doing so much, gaze fixed on me. I wished he'd go back to the garage to do whatever he did out there instead of focusing all his attention on me.

His jaw was clenched tight, the little muscle jumping up and down in what looked like barely controlled anger. "Explain."

I set one foot into the kitchen, then another, careful not to make any sudden movements. "The coffee machine or your constant foul mood?"

His eyes narrowed. Okay, not the right time to be a smart-ass. But there was still time to salvage this. I had great reasons for buying it. Okay, one great reason. "Everyone loves coffee. We can now offer coffee to customers while they are waiting, or during meetings. If you have a slow month, we can sell it." And just to make sure he got my original point, I repeated, "Everyone loves coffee."

"You didn't think to check with me before you purchased a coffee machine worth two thousand dollars?" The vein on his neck looked like it was going to jump at me any second.

"But it was a bargain. They are usually over four grand. I saved you two thousand dollars." How did he not understand this? It was simple math.

"I could have saved four thousand dollars if you hadn't even bought it. We don't need a coffee machine. Return it."

Both my hands were clutched tightly around my mug, and I hoped what I was about to tell him wouldn't make his head explode. "Well, there might be a teeny tiny problem with that. Because you see, when it's a highly discounted item, they don't accept returns." The last part was said in a rush, and I was inching closer to the door. Admittedly, I should have thought this whole thing through a bit more. But who would have thought he wouldn't be happy with a brand-new coffee machine at half price? Everyone loved coffee.

He noticed my retreat and stomped closer. "Where are you going?"

"Me? Nowhere." I tried to sound innocent, but it came out more like a squeak.

"Stay where you are. We are not done here."

My feet had other ideas and continued to move backward ever so slowly. I was close to freedom.

"Can't we just agree to disagree?"

"Agree to disagree? Are you fucking with me? You just cost me a lot of money. Since you didn't ask me if you could buy the machine, and I would never have approved the purchase, I refuse to pay for it. I guess you'll be here a bit longer than you thought. This time working off a coffee machine."

My feet stopped in shock. "What? You can't do that. I did you a favor, and I know you can afford it. You are making a lot of money. You are so far in the black you could buy an island. A small country. Disneyland. How amazing would it be to own Disneyland? Or a castle, then you could—"

I was too busy thinking of the things he could buy to notice his approach. When I blinked and remembered I was supposed to make a run for it, he was in front of me. The first thing I noticed was his smell. I loved the soap he used. I should ask him about it. The second thing I noticed was the tight line of his mouth. A mouth that was normally nice and full. The third thing was his eyes that were blazing fire. Very pretty fire, but fire nevertheless. My mouth went dry and shut instantly. At least I hoped it was closed.

"I don't want to buy Disneyland."

"Then how about an island? You really do need a holiday. A few months on the beach would loosen you up a bit."

"I don't waste my money on bullshit. That's why I have it. I will add the two grand to your debt. If you keep this shit up, you'll be working here for the rest of your life."

I knew I had lost when his right eye started twitching. That definitely wasn't a good sign, and for once in my life, I shut up. He brushed past me and stalked out of the room. So much for making friends with coffee. He acted like I offered him salad.

The rest of the day went marginally better. I sulked for a bit, then made more coffee, which the guys loved. When I had sufficiently licked my wounds, I started on the work schedule.

I made everyone write down their booked appointments and transferred them onto a spreadsheet on the computer. I didn't dare talk to Jameson, but at least I got everyone else. They also explained to me how long they would need for each job so I could assign them accordingly. By the time I entered all the current jobs, my eyes were blurry and I could feel a headache coming on. I dreaded riding my bike home.

The door opened, and I lifted my tired head from the pile of papers it was resting on. "Honeycakes. Got something for you," Landon said and shook a set of keys in front of my face.

"You fixed my car?"

He dropped the keys in my hand and nodded. "I fixed your car."

"You are my hero," I exclaimed and hugged him. "Does that mean I get to drive it home? No more riding the devil mobile?"

"I just had to replace your spark plugs and radiator. Also did your oil change and you need new tires. But, yes, you're good to drive it without risking your life."

"I'm so happy right now." I released him and, yes, clapped my hands. "How much do I owe you?"

Landon's mouth twitched, and he grinned at me. "Nothing. All on us."

I blinked once, twice, and when he was still there, I asked, "How?"

"You are part of the team now. We look out for each other. And that means we all pitch in when it comes to fixing your car. The parts were cheap, and it didn't take long to replace them. Jameson would never let you pay."

I was so happy I felt tears spring into my eyes. I wasn't used to handouts.

"Why are you crying?" Landon held up his hands and cast a panicked glance at the door. "I thought this was a good thing."

"It is a good thing," I mumbled through my tears.

He stumbled backward. "I should get back to work." This was accompanied by another frantic look at the door. He wanted to get away from my puddle face but was too polite to just bolt. "Are you going to be okay?" he asked, the panic in his voice evident.

"I'm fine." I wasn't fine, which was proven when I started crying in earnest. And then came the hiccups. Big fat tears were running down my cheeks. "Just so grateful."

The door opened again, and through the haze of my tears I saw Jameson. Humiliation seemed to be my trusted companion these days. He was the last person I wanted to see me cry.

"The fuck did you do?" he shouted at Landon whose eyes were still trained at the door.

"Nothing, man. I told her the car was done, and she started crying."

"Out," Jameson barked, and Landon tripped over his own feet in his haste to do just that.

Jameson turned me around to face him, his hands on my shoulders. "Why the tears?" he asked, his tone gentle.

I sniffled, grateful the hiccups were gone. "I take care of myself. Always have."

"We didn't try to take away your independence. We just wanted to help."

The tears kept falling, and I swiped at them, frantic to make them stop. I heard a loud inhale and a muttered curse, and then I found myself crushed against Jameson's chest.

"If you tell the guys about this, I'm going to make you clean the toilets for a month," he said into my hair, his voice gruff.

I buried my head in his chest and put my arms around him, holding on as if my life depended on it. And maybe it did.

He whispered gentle words and stroked my back. We just stood there, me sniffling into his shirt, him holding me patiently. I guess he wasn't scared off by tears. And was I seriously hugging Jameson? Did I fall asleep at the desk again? If I did, this was a damn good dream. And if it was a dream, that meant dream Jameson wouldn't mind if my hands wandered a bit lower.

I had almost made it to my destination when he squeezed me tighter. "Stop right there." Dream Jameson was as much fun as real Jameson. I should probably let go anyway before I started humping his leg.

With one last inhale, I peeled myself off his comfortable chest. "I'm sorry about losing it like that. It's just that this is the nicest thing anyone has ever done for me."

He swiped his thumb across my cheek, wiping away the last of my tears. "I gotta get back to work."

And he was gone. I stood in the silent office, wondering if it had been a dream after all.

9

"You coming tonight?" Clay asked. He was leaning on my desk and drinking the cup of coffee I had made him earlier. Jameson and Landon had both been avoiding me for the rest of the week, pretty much sprinting out of the room as soon as I walked in.

I eventually cornered Landon in the kitchen when he was too desperate for a coffee to pay attention to his surroundings. After many promises to never cry in front of him again and make him coffee, he ruffled my hair and stopped bolting out the door every time he saw me.

"What's tonight?" I asked.

"We meet up at Elmar's every Friday. Kind of a team thing, so when I asked you if you were coming, I shouldn't have phrased it as a question because it really wasn't."

I counted the hours of sleep I would get if I came along. Maybe if I left early I would be able to get some rest before I had to be at Sweet Dreams tomorrow morning. I was supposed to be off tomorrow, but the two staff members Rayna had were off sick. After many threats and the promise to cook me dinner every day next week, I agreed to come in. If I was being honest, I would have helped her out either way, she was my favorite aunt after all. But dinner was an added bonus.

I guess I could swing by for a bit and still be able to get up tomorrow. "Sure, I'll drop in."

Looking happy with my response, he tipped his chin in my direction and went back out to the garage.

I got lost in work for a few hours and didn't notice when Landon came back.

"Time to shut down your computer, honeycakes. The boys already left. You're with me," he said, pushing my chair to the side. He leaned over my keyboard and studied the screen. "How do you turn this thing off?" He stretched his body up and over the desk, trying to find the button.

"You looking for dust behind there?" I fought the laugh that threatened to bubble out of me.

He shot me an annoyed look. "Just turn it off so we can go."

I did as I was told, making sure to throw him a grin, and followed him out the door. He locked up after me, and I noticed I didn't have a key for the door. "How come I didn't get a key? What if I want to come in super early? Or stay back?"

"If you make it past the four-week mark, you'll get one."

I was definitely going to stay past the four weeks, whether I wanted to or not. And my debt had grown instead of getting smaller, so I would be here for a while.

"Care to make a bet?" I asked.

"What are you offering?"

"If I make it past the four-week mark, you have to tell Jameson that it was you who broke the fridge door."

Landon made a face as if he'd bitten into a lemon.

"Awww, come on, that's not fair. It was an accident. And I stuck it back together."

"With masking tape. It's so obvious. And once he finds out, he's going to be on everyone's ass until someone fesses up. If you just admit to it, we'll all be saved from the Spanish Inquisition."

And I would also get to watch Jameson yell at someone else for a change. Evil? Maybe. But hey, I never said I was a nice person. Anything to take the attention away from me was welcome.

Landon raised his brows at me. "And what do I get if I win?"

"I'll wash your car for a month."

He seemed to consider this for a moment before he spoke again. "Only if you do it in your bikini."

I could do that. There was no way I'd lose. I held out my hand. "You're on."

We shook on it and got into Landon's car. He insisted on driving me, and since I took every opportunity not to have to sit in my rust bucket, I gladly accepted.

I soon found out that Landon was a full-blown "I don't stop for old people or kids" maniac. He drove like he was late for dinner and his mom made cherry pie. A little fact about Landon I found out early on: he would do most things for cherry pie.

He squealed around every corner, cut off more people than I could be asked to count, and made me grip the seat so hard my fingers went numb. When we finally made it to Elmar's, he was as happy as ever, and I was shaky from watching him nearly kill a few pedestrians and a bird.

I stumbled out of his car, holding on to the frame for

dear life. My knees were shaking, and I took a deep breath.

"What's wrong with you?" he asked. "You look a little green around the nose."

I flipped him off and walked toward the big brick building, my eyes flying from the bikes outside to the customers standing near the door. I hesitated, not sure if I should go inside or cut my losses and take a cab home. Trouble liked me a little too much, and I really shouldn't go looking for it in a place like that. I never had much luck in biker bars.

Landon noticed my hesitation and put his arm around me. "Don't be a chicken. It's a great bar. They make the best nachos. Nothing is going to happen to you in there. Trust me. And Jameson is friends with the owner."

"Don't know what surprises me more. That Jameson has a friend or that he is a biker at heart."

Landon guided me inside, and I was surprised at the cozy interior. Leather chairs, dim lighting, and mahogany floors made up the main part of the bar. We walked past groups of bikers who all called out to him in greeting, which he returned with a nod. A huge bar took up the middle of the room. The furniture on the other side looked much the same, only some of the seats were couches.

"The guys are over there," Landon said, pointing at a booth tucked in the corner.

I scooted onto the bench next to Clay, and Landon pulled up a chair at the end of the table.

"Finally," Mason complained. "I'm starving, and J made us wait for you."

"Got here as fast as we could, but there was a speed camera on Burton, so had to slow down," Landon said.

Him slowing down meant stepping on his brakes so abruptly I was thrown forward in my seat, and his tires screeched in protest, followed by rapid acceleration as soon as we were past.

I punched his arm and scowled at him. "You nearly killed me. I was writing my last will two seconds after we pulled away from Drake's. There is no way I'm ever getting in a car with you again."

The waitress came around, interrupting my rant, and put her hand on Landon's arm. "Laney," she exclaimed and thrust her ample cleavage in his face. He didn't seem to mind at all, and I shook my head at his ogling. She was pushing her duck lips into some kind of pout, as far as they would allow her to anyway. It was working if she was going for the surprised sex doll look. "You didn't call me last week."

"Sorry, honey. Lost your number. How about we get reacquainted after dinner?" He winked at her and placed his order. I made a gagging noise next to him, and he put his hand on my leg and squeezed in warning. I nearly jumped out of my seat at the sudden invasion.

When he refused to let go, I tried prying his hands off me, but he held on strong. "Let go, Laney," I hissed under my breath.

He eased his grip. "Only if you promise to be a good girl and stop with the judgment. And don't call me Laney."

After another failed attempt at removing his giant claws, I gave in. "Fine," I hissed.

He released my leg, and I rubbed the spot he had manhandled. Bastard. He was going to pay for that.

The waitress was looking at me and I frowned, unsure what she wanted. Clay nudged me and said, "What do you want for dinner?"

Right, dinner, the reason we came here in the first place. I hadn't even looked at the menu. "Do you have burgers?"

"Of course we do," she said, her face telling me she thought the question was stupid. "You want fries too?"

"Sure. Thanks."

Jameson was sitting on the other side of the booth talking to Mason, and I couldn't help but study his profile.

Landon nudged me out of my moment of weakness and leaned in close. "What are you doin', honeycakes?"

His voice startled me, and I jumped out of my seat in surprise. I knocked into Clay who spilled his beer all over his shirt.

I was too busy ogling Jameson to notice Clay's narrowed eyes. A hand on my arm interrupted my obsessive stare. "Are you finally going to realize that he is a good guy and make lots of pretty babies together? Because I'm ready to become an uncle."

I choked on my own spit and turned all my attention to Landon. "What the fuck, what? I mean fuck what?" My inability to form a coherent sentence did not exactly help my case.

I got up and out of his reach before I dug my hole any deeper. Unfortunately, my sudden movement put me in the path of a biker that was walking past our table. Fuck my life, but what bad juju was this? I must have seriously pissed off someone to have all this shit coming my way.

Maybe it was the baking pan I nicked from Rayna last week and didn't tell her about. I knew I shouldn't have done that.

The biker I accidently punched in the guts looked murderous, and he was big. As in *he eats little kids for break-*

fast and loves to throw big logs around in his free time. I scooted back in my seat. "I'm so sorry," I stuttered, my eyes huge saucers, too afraid to blink.

"What the hell is wrong with you, bitch?" He was definitely not taking this well.

"No-Nothing." I knew I walked into him, but hey, look at the size of me compared to him.

He grabbed me roughly out of the booth, and I yelped. "I spilled my drink because of you."

"So-Sorry." I tried again, but if anything he looked even angrier. My feet were dangling off the ground, and I was going to wet myself if he didn't release me soon. I could feel my bladder weakening by the second.

My chest was struggling with the effort to pull air into my lungs. I was going to die. This was it. I waited for my life to flash before my eyes, but nothing happened. Instead I was pulled back against a hard chest, and scary biker dude let go of me. He looked over my shoulder and nodded his chin.

"Jameson. She belongs to you?"

"She does. And I don't appreciate you putting your hands on her."

Biker dude put up said hands and stepped back. I sank into Jameson in relief, and he pulled me closer. My legs were shaky, and if I didn't have someone holding on to me as tightly as Jameson was right now, I was sure I would end up in a heap on the floor.

"She punched me."

"It was clearly an accident. I definitely heard her say she was sorry."

"Keep a shorter leash on her, or the next guy she assaults won't be as understanding as me."

Did he just call himself understanding?

"Not your problem. Now, are we done here?" Jameson's voice allowed for no argument. He was scary big and scary angry all the time, and they clearly knew all about his temper here.

Biker dude stepped back. "We're done." He turned on his heel and was swallowed up in the crowd.

I wasn't moving. Why wasn't I moving? Right, because I was still being held by Jameson. He didn't seem to be in a hurry to let me go either, so we just stood there. I felt the guys' eyes on me and turned to a table full of concerned faces. Mason was half out of his seat, and Landon was standing behind us, looking ready to take someone's head off.

"Fucking Mack," he said and got back into his seat. His move seemed to pull everyone out of their frozen states. Conversation continued, and Landon joked around like he wasn't ready to kill someone just a few seconds ago.

"You all right?" Jameson asked, his cheek pressed against my head, his mouth on my ear.

I only managed a weak nod. Why did I even come here? I always make a mess of things. Tonight was the perfect example.

Jameson squeezed me to get my attention. "He won't bother you again."

I nodded again. He didn't let go of me as he turned me around and guided me back into the booth and got in next to me. Everyone shuffled up, and I ended up wedged between Clay and Jameson.

I knew it was a mistake coming out tonight. Jameson carried on as if nothing had happened and didn't acknowledge my presence once. He was pressed against me, the heat of his body penetrating every pore of mine. I was getting hot and restless. Dinner was a welcome reprieve and gave me something to do with my hands.

I scarfed down my burger, nearly choking a few times in my haste. I ignored the fries and got up, still chewing my last bite. "Thanks for dinner, guys, but I gotta go. See you all on Monday."

Amidst the protests of me leaving so soon, Jameson got up to let me out. I did an awkward half wave at him and walked away. He followed close behind. Too close, since he kept brushing up against me.

"What are you doing?" I asked and stopped.

He put a hand on my back and started walking again, taking me with him. "Taking you home."

"Right. But I can take a cab."

He grunted in answer, and I shut up and let him drive me home. We didn't say one word to each other the entire way.

10

It was Monday, and I was depressed. I spent all day Saturday working, and after my shift, Rayna dropped me at Drake's to get my car. Sunday was a write-off after I had to help Dad clean his yard when his neighbors complained about the smell, something that happened frequently, but he only reacted when he was sent an official letter, aka grounds management told him to pick up his shit. My weekend had been gone in a flash, and I was back to work.

Maisie and Stella had left for the summer, Maisie going to London for an internship and Stella to help out at her parents' farm. Life sucked.

"Willa, open the door. I know you're in there," Landon said, his voice muffled by the locked kitchen door.

Can't a girl eat cupcakes in peace? "I'm eating lunch. Go away."

"I know it was you who put that fucking glitter shit in my air vents. Do you have any idea how hard it was to get out?"

"That was kind of the point," I mumbled through

the bite I had just taken out of the red velvet cupcake I made that morning. Delicious. And it almost made me forget that my friends were gone, I had to work three jobs, and Jameson was back to not talking to me. Almost forgot, but not quite. Another two or three cupcakes should do the job and cause me to have temporary memory loss thanks to sugar overload.

"This isn't over," he bellowed.

I ignored him and picked up cupcake number four. Still had three to get through and refused to be disturbed until I was done. His retreating footsteps put a smile on my face. Another win for yours truly.

And the glitter was only in retaliation for the spider he put on my desk. I was terrified of spiders. If I had the choice between sleeping in a bed with a spider or poison ivy, the choice would be obvious, and I wouldn't pick the spider.

So when I came in that morning and found a giant spider crawling all over my screen, I lost my shit. Literally lost it. But no, that wasn't the low point of my morning. Not by a long shot. As I was screaming bloody murder and ran out the office door, Jameson came sprinting down his stairs in nothing but his boxers. You'd think that would be something to make my day a whole lot better. It would be if that was where the story ended.

But he was an absolute dick about it. I didn't think he understood the gravity of the spider situation.

"What now?" Jameson asked. His voice was scratchy from sleep, and I was staring at his chest. And I mean, who wouldn't? It was the chest every other chest should take as an example. My hands itched to touch it, but I managed to ball them into fists and clench them at my sides. There would definitely be no touching in their future.

I felt incredibly stupid for screaming like I was being murdered. But then again, the spider was pretty big. It might have been really hungry, or maybe it was just having a bad day and that was reason enough to bite me. My life was in danger. Retreating back into the office, rather facing off with hairy legs than barely dressed and angry jackass, I said, "I'm good. Just peachy. Downright dandy. Marvelous. Fantastic. Ha—"

"Okay, I get it, you're fine," Jameson cut off my ramble. "Then why did you scream?"

"Spider," I replied and pointed at my desk. The hairy beast was still taking a walk around my keyboard.

Jameson casually strolled over and picked it up. I shrieked and took a step back and then one forward. I wanted to save him but wasn't brave enough to get closer. "Save yourself and drop it while you can," I yelled, still jumping back and forth, unsure if I should get the hell out of there or save Jameson.

"Ralph isn't going to eat anyone." He held the beast up to his face. "How the hell did you get out?"

"You're on a first-name basis with that thing?"

"It's Ralph. He lives in the terrarium next to Mason's work station."

Jameson walked into the garage, and I followed at a safe distance. I watched him set the hairy clump into a terrarium and close the lid. "Okay, who was it?" Jameson asked the guys who had all congregated when they saw us come in.

Nobody said anything, but I saw Landon try to contain his snicker. I made a slashing gesture against my throat and stomped back into the office. He was going to pay. And pay he did. The glitter was a brilliant idea. Thanks, YouTube.

A creak sounded above my head, and I looked up at

the window above the kitchen cabinets. The latch turned and it opened. Landon squeezed himself through the small gap, his face red from exertion.

"Seriously?" I asked through cupcake crumbs while gaping at him.

He landed on top of the cupboards, and I was afraid they were going to give out under his weight. He managed not to plunge to his death but instead swung his legs around and landed on the counter. From there, he jumped down and was standing next to me with a triumphant grin. I had to grudgingly admit that I was impressed.

"You didn't think you were going to eat all the cupcakes by yourself, did you?"

I watched him take two cupcakes, one for each hand and eat them in two bites. "A man with many talents," I said and tried to defend the last cupcake.

He was faster and swiped it off the table before I had a chance to get to it. The whole thing went into his mouth.

"Now to the matter at hand," he said once he was done swallowing his bounty. "Why are you holed up in this smelly kitchen instead of eating lunch outside with us like you have done since you started working here?" He took another look at me, and his eyes went wide. Here we go. I should have just stayed at home.

"What happened to your hair?"

I put my hands over said hair to cover it and glared at Landon. "That's the worst thing you could say to a girl."

Instead of backing off and letting me wallow in my misery, he leaned over the table and pulled my hands away. "It looks like you got a haircut. A really bad one."

I slapped him away and brushed my hands over my

hair to straighten it out. If I pushed it down just right, you couldn't tell that some of it was shorter than the rest. "My hairdryer exploded on me this morning, and the selfish bastard took a few of my hairs with him on his way to hell. Now shut up and finish your cupcake."

Landon wrinkled his forehead and examined me some more. "I would recommend a hat. Or a wig."

I flipped him off and braided it instead. Lucky for me, the short bits were just long enough to fit.

"That works too," he said once I finished.

Defeated with life, I hung my head and hoped he wouldn't tell anyone. Instead of leaving me to my misery, he pulled me off the chair and outside to eat with the guys. To my surprise, he didn't say a word about my hair and only looked at it a few times.

11

The guys managed to cheer me up, and I felt better about life. Maybe it was time to suck it up and take charge. I was ready, I was pumped, and I would make life my bitch. No more sad sack Willa who was scared of spiders and hairdryers. Maybe tomorrow I'd even take a look into the terrarium without freaking out. Or it could wait until next week. I was a new and improved version of myself.

The positive thoughts lasted until my phone beeped. Lately any sound coming from it wasn't a good omen. Unfortunately, this time wasn't an exception.

Dad: *Honey, can you come pick me up? Got into a little situation in Vegas.*

I stared at my phone, dread rising in my stomach. The text message didn't bode well for me. I hoped this was one of the nightmares I tended to have. I would wake up any minute. I was sure Dad wouldn't do this to me again, especially not now when I was still working off his last debt.

I typed out a reply.

Me: *Where are you?*

I put the phone down, and after eating the last bit of my chocolate bar, I started pacing the office. It was afternoon. If I left now, I could make it to Vegas by midnight. If my car made it that far without breaking down on me.

The door to the garage opened, and Jameson came through. "Who died?" he asked when he saw my pained expression.

"Nobody died." I stopped my trek through the office and shuffled some papers around. "How can I help you?"

"You can start by telling me what's wrong." His arms were crossed over his chest, legs wide, brows raised.

I shook my head and abandoned the papers. "It's nothing. Really. I'm just overreacting."

"You mean like when Landon put Ralph in here?"

"That was in no way an overreaction. He put a spider on my desk, a humongous living spider with hairy everything."

"Ralph would never hurt you. He's old and lazy."

"Well, I didn't know that before he put the damn thing in my office. And he knew full well I was going to freak." I narrowed my eyes in my best death stare, but he just continued to look at me with his stupid eyes and his stupid hair that was all over the place.

My phone started ringing. It was Dad.

"Honey," he said when I picked up, pointedly ignoring Jameson who made himself comfortable on the edge of my desk.

"Dad. Finally. Where the hell are you?"

There was an embarrassed cough down the line, and it sounded like he dropped the phone. "Sorry, I'm back."

"What did you do?"

"I didn't do anything, but I may need a new car."

I groaned into the phone and rubbed my forehead. Not again. "Tell me you didn't gamble everything away again."

"Okay, I won't then."

I cursed silently and kicked the desk. "Where are you?"

"At Greg's. I need you to come pick me up."

Of course he did. Because he didn't think I had a life and might be busy. And he would have no money left for the bus or train.

"Fine. I can be there in a few hours."

"I can stay here tonight but need to be out by tomorrow."

"I'll leave tonight. Keep your phone close."

"Thanks, honey. See you soon. Love you."

"Love you too, Dad."

As much as I hated what he did to me, I still loved him.

We hung up, and I threw my phone against the wall. It bounced off the plaster, leaving a big mark behind. It was covered in the world's hardest case since I had a habit of dropping it on hard surfaces and into water. I was 99 percent sure it wasn't broken. The same couldn't be said about the wall.

Throwing things wasn't enough so I stomped my foot and kicked my office chair. As soon as I made contact, pain shot up my leg and I yelped. I held my foot and jumped up and down on one leg. What a mess. I didn't feel better at all. Violence solved nothing. And now I had to fix a hole in a wall as well.

"That didn't sound like a little Ralph overreaction," Jameson said, ignoring my tantrum. I had forgotten that he was there.

"Would you mind if I took off a little earlier today?" I asked.

"Where are you going?"

"Vegas."

"You are going to Vegas by yourself? I don't think so."

"It's not like I'm going there for fun. I have to get—" The door shut, and I was talking to an empty room. And I guess that was a yes to the early finish.

And since he was so agreeable to me going, I turned off my computer and headed out the door.

And I was indeed going. Just not the way I imagined. Somehow I found myself sitting in Jameson's truck. With Jameson, who insisted on driving me there. Once I left the office, he was waiting for me outside. Apparently the two minutes it took to get ready to go was enough time for him to pull his truck around and let the guys know that he'd be gone for the weekend.

He used my confusion to his advantage and guided me onto the seat, not giving me a chance to protest. At least we stopped at my apartment to grab what I needed for an overnight trip.

I was only allowed ten minutes of frantically throwing things into a backpack before Jameson stomped through the door. "What's taking so long? If we want to make it to Vegas before tomorrow morning, we gotta go."

He peered into my backpack. "Please tell me we won't need the flashlight." His hand disappeared inside the bag. "And a rope? What the hell would we need scissors for?"

I snatched my stuff from him and crammed it back inside the overflowing backpack. I remembered the candles, hairpins, and Taser, but where was the first aid kit? Right, kitchen drawer where I left it after Maisie hit her head when she tried to jump over my couch. Emphasis on the word "tried."

Dad and Vegas never mixed well, and I had to be prepared, hence the overflowing backpack.

I barely had time to grab my jacket before Jameson grabbed my hand and pulled me out of my apartment.

He took my backpack and threw it onto his back seat. "Why do you look like you just found out the Spice Girls broke up?" he asked.

I glared at him. "Because I love Sporty Spice?"

He opened the passenger door and motioned for me to get in. "So what's your dad doing in Vegas?"

I was hoping to be able to avoid the question for a bit longer and said, "Picking up an Elvis statue?"

Jameson closed my door and got in behind the wheel but didn't start the truck. Instead he gave me an impassive face. This was a stare off I couldn't win, unless winning meant jumping on his lap. Because that I could do.

I studied my hands and tried again. "Dying to see Cirque de Soleil?" Maybe I should stop making my answers sound like questions. "He wanted to visit the Eiffel Tower." There it was. A statement. I could totally do this.

"Willa," Jameson drew out my name, sounding like he was talking to a two-year-old. "I heard you on the phone. Tell me what's going on so I can help you."

"It's nothing. Really."

"Why do you think I insisted on coming along?"

I gave him a "duh, I'm not stupid" look. "Because you really want to go to Vegas."

"Nope. Because you clearly need my help. Do you

really think your sorry excuse for a car would have made it the five hundred miles?"

I knew he was right. I barely made it the twenty miles to get to work. "Look, I'm grateful for the ride, but I can take care of myself. I don't need your help." He turned the key in the ignition, and the engine came to life.

"Well, you've got it, whether you want it or not. Now try telling me again why we're going to Vegas." He was relentless. And I was so used to taking care of myself that I didn't know what to think of his help. Did I like it? Not sure. Was I secretly grateful for the support even though he didn't really know what he was supporting? Unfortunately, the answer to that one was yes.

"I have to pick up my dad because he gambled his car away." My voice was so low, I wasn't sure if he heard me over the hum of the engine and the radio playing in the background. I was ashamed. Dad was my family, but I wished he made better choices. Preferably ones that didn't end up with him getting arrested or losing his car.

"Okay. Let's do it." Jameson sounded like we were going for ice cream, not trying to drag my irresponsible, stuck-in-his-twenties dad home. He pulled away from the curb and just like that we were on our way to Vegas.

I had to swallow hard to dislodge the lump stuck in my throat. All this niceness was making me break out in hives. I could feel my neck getting itchy. And my eyes. But that might be the tears that were trying to break free. *Not happening, you weak little fools. You're staying confined in my eyeballs where you belong.*

A tattooed arm appeared in my vision and his hand settled on my knee. His touch burned a hole into my skin. "You should have told me straight away."

"It's not your problem."

"What if I want to make it my problem?"

"Then you're a fool who has clearly never had to pick up a Montgomery in Vegas before."

"Can't say I've ever had the pleasure."

There really wasn't anything I could say other than thank you. Without Jameson, I would probably not have made it to Vegas. It also saved me from driving for six hours. There was no way I would stay at Greg's for the night. He was one of Dad's friends that I avoided as much as possible.

I glanced at Jameson, who was now concentrating on the road, and felt a familiar tingling in my stomach. The more time I spent with him, the more I started to realize what all the fuss was about. He was a good guy. Rude, but not heartless. And I was the fool who had just joined his fan club.

Jameson drove the whole way there. I offered to take over a few times, but he said he was fine whenever I mentioned it.

We didn't talk much, and I fell asleep after asking him for the third time if he wanted me to drive. Might as well sleep when I could—who knew when I would get the chance again? The gentle brush of a hand on my face woke me up. "Willa."

I dragged myself into a sitting position after ending up slumped against the window. Jameson was leaning over me, his hand still on my cheek. "You up?"

"Mmmhmm."

"I got you some coffee at the last rest stop. Might be a bit co—"

I didn't let him finish his sentence before I grabbed the cup he held out and gulped down half its contents. The coffee was lukewarm and tasted bitter, but I was so grateful to get any at all that I didn't care. I put the cup down and smiled at Jameson. "You got me coffee."

"That I did. If I'd known cheap gas station coffee was all it would take for you to smile at me, I'd have bought some sooner."

We were parked at a rest stop just outside of Vegas. Jameson was sitting in the driver's seat and held out a bag. "I got you a sandwich as well. Wasn't sure what you liked, so I got a few different ones. I'll eat whatever you don't want."

I stared at him for a moment and took the bag to look inside. I selected one and handed the rest back to him. "Thanks. You didn't have to do that."

"I know."

I unwrapped my sandwich and took a big bite. Ham and cheese with mustard, one of my favorites. Jameson ate two sandwiches while I finished mine before he started the truck and pulled back out onto the highway. "Where to?"

"Dad's staying with a friend in Summerlin."

"Summerlin it is."

We drove the rest of the way in comfortable silence. I was anxious to get this whole ordeal over with. I sent Dad a text that I was almost there, but he didn't reply.

Greg lived in a neglected condo that had seen better days. He had never held a job but managed to keep his head above water by working all sorts of shady jobs and not asking questions. The dodgy business must be paying well because I spotted a brand-new Mustang in his car bay.

Jameson parked out on the street and opened his door. I didn't want him to witness any of what was sure to go down. This was embarrassing enough already, no need to keep driving it home. "I'll be right back," I said, desperate to get him to stay in the truck.

He put a hand on my arm, stopping me from getting out. "No, you're not. I'm coming with you."

"There's really no need. It will only take a few minutes."

He ignored my protest and got out of the truck. Exhaling a deep breath, I slid out of my seat and joined him. He was already waiting outside my door and took my hand, ignoring my weak protest.

Greg was in the bottom condo, so at least we didn't have to climb any stairs. The music was blasting from inside, and I sighed. It was after midnight, and they would be tanked. Great. Dad would be a pain to get out of there.

I knocked and waited, rolling on the balls of my feet. Back and forth. Back and forth. In between fidgeting, I shot nervous glances over my shoulder at Jameson. He was an immovable wall behind me, watching my every move. Nobody answered, and I knocked again, this time harder.

The door swung open, revealing a mountain of a man I didn't recognize. He had a shaved head and was tattooed up to his neck. I automatically took a step back.

"You Cindy?"

"Who?"

He looked me up and down and spoke extra slowly. "Cindy. The stripper."

Jameson growled and stepped forward, but before he got very far, I pushed in front of him. "Fuck no. I'm here for Garret Montgomery."

Door guy nodded and stepped back. "Last time I saw him, he was playing poker with Greg."

I walked past him, Jameson glued to my side, my

hand firmly held in his. Greg's friends were pigs, and the less interaction I had with them the better. Having someone next to me put me at ease, especially since that person was Jameson. I realized I trusted him completely and was glad he was there. Mountain man didn't try to touch me but instead closed the door and nodded in the direction of the living room. "Try in there."

We walked into the hazy room, filled with cigarette smoke and weed. It was hard to see much of anything, but we made our way in the direction he indicated. Dad was easy to spot, his blond head standing out.

I stopped next to him, but he didn't even look up. No surprise there since he didn't see anything or anyone else once he started a game, but there was no way I'd stick around. Especially not after Greg noticed me. "Little Montgomery. Come over here and say hello."

His obvious perusal of my body made me want to cover myself in bleach before getting the hell out of there, even if it meant leaving Dad behind. Jameson stepped close, pressing his front to the side of my body.

I looked at Greg, not even managing the tiniest of smiles. He was a disgusting leech who tried to feel me up when I was sixteen.

"Greg," I said, my voice tight.

"Garret, my man, why didn't you tell me your daughter had grown into such a hot piece of ass? We could have worked something out about your debt."

I felt Jameson tense beside me, the hold he had on my hand becoming uncomfortable. The comment finally made Dad look up and notice me. "Willa. What are you doing here?" He looked confused, as if he hadn't called me hours earlier.

"I'm here to pick you up. Come on, we need to go."

"Honey, I need to finish the game." His bloodshot

eyes met mine, and I watched him sway in his seat. Shit. He was beyond tanked.

I took his arm, trying to get him to stand. "Dad, come on. Let's go."

Greg watched us with his beady little rat eyes. Any attention was bad attention when it came to him. We had to get out of here.

I managed a glimpse at Dad's cards when he lifted them off the table and my heart sank. He was definitely not going to win this round unless he was a great bluffer, which he definitely wasn't. His inebriated state didn't do much for his poker face, either.

"Your father here owes me money, Willa. He can't just walk out. This game is his chance to get it all back."

"He's drunk out of his mind. You're fucking playing him like you play everyone else. Let us go, and I'll pay you back whatever he owes you."

Greg clicked his tongue, his eyes on my chest. "That's not how it works, and you know it. Give me the money and you can go... after the game is finished, of course."

I was an idiot for even considering it, but I was also desperate. And desperate Willa made stupid decisions. "Let me take his place."

Jameson pulled me around to face him. "Not happening. You are not putting yourself at risk for him."

I freed my hand and put space between us. "Not your decision. I'm a big girl and know what I'm getting myself into. Now you can support me and be there for me, or you can wait outside."

His face was a mask of barely controlled anger. The muscles in his jaw started ticking, and I knew I'd won. Without another word, I turned around, ignoring the fire shooting out of his eyes.

I hadn't played in a few years, but Dad had taught me well. Poker was all I'd played growing up. It was the only time he actually showed interest in me, and I'd soaked up every bit of information he divulged. I knew I was a good player, but his hand was terrible. I had to start a new game for a chance to win.

"What do I get out of it?" Greg asked.

"Someone you can actually play with? Don't think I didn't notice you just making calls for Dad because he's too out of it to do it himself."

Greg liked a good challenge. And if I was able to give him enough of an incentive, I was sure he'd go for it. My skin crawled at the thought of having to sit opposite him, but this was for Dad. No way would I just walk out the door without him.

He grinned, too excited about my offer. I had a bad feeling. "I'll stop the game right now and let your dad off the hook if you step in. But the stakes will change. If you win, I'll erase your dad's debt and you are free to go. If you lose, I'll get *you*."

The revulsion was hard to mask. He was one sick and twisted man. Who knew what him *getting me* meant.

"Willa," Jameson growled behind me. I ignored his attempts to get me to turn around again, instead thinking that of all the times Dad had screwed up, this one was by far the worst.

Greg cheated at every game. Sometimes it was obvious, other times it was impossible to catch him. My options looked bleak: play in a game that was most likely rigged or walk away and leave Dad with his mess. If history told me anything, it was that I had never walked away and wouldn't do so now. We were family after all.

"You erase Dad's debt even if I lose?"

His smirk was of someone who knew they'd won. "I will. And to make it easy, we'll play countdown."

I groaned. Was I ready to place my fate into the hands of destiny? I guess I was because I nodded and took a deep breath of stale cigarette smoke and weed. The smell of champions. "You get one night."

"Two. Garret has quite the debt to me. Doesn't know when to quit."

Didn't I know it? But I also knew there was no way I'd survive more than one night. And even that was a stretch. "No. It's one night or we don't have a deal."

His eyes held mine for a few seconds before travelling over my boobs. I would definitely need that bleach later. Apparently happy with what he saw, he nodded. "Fine."

We shook hands, and I resisted the urge to wipe my palms on my pants before sitting down in Dad's place who we'd moved to the couch. No need to poke an already aggravated asshole. Jameson was standing as close as he could get, his presence reassuring, even though the anger was coming off him in waves.

Well, at least my voice sounded a lot surer than my wildly fluttering heart. I was so screwed. I started out with a shit hand and things didn't improve. There was also no way to bluff my way out because we both had to show our hands at the end. I had to face it. I made bad choices all the time. Some worse than others. Some monumentally stupid. Like this one. I pretty much signed over my dignity and body to a disgusting, vile man who would do everything he could to ruin me in the time he had.

And judging by the man currently crowding me and growling in my ear, I had also majorly pissed Jameson off. I just hoped for once I was lucky and didn't screw this up. A glance over my shoulder confirmed he looked ready to tear someone apart, most likely Greg. Resigned, I turned back to my cards.

We were on the last round, I had the choice to exchange one card or stay with the mediocre hand I was currently holding. One card could change everything. I nodded and accepted another card to exchange for one of mine.

Greg nodded at me, and we both turned our cards around. I glanced at my hand and stopped breathing. I had four of a kind. I jerked my head up and saw his full house. No way. I had won.

I couldn't tear my eyes away from the cards. They flitted from mine to Greg's and back, making sure I really had the better hand. There was no way he didn't cheat. Maybe he just didn't think I had a chance of anything better than a full house.

"Get out of my sight," Greg roared. He stood up and gripped the table so hard his knuckles turned white. I was too stunned to move, but Jameson didn't have the same problem. He pulled me out of my chair and a safe distance away before the whole table crashed to the floor upside down.

Someone had anger issues. I rushed to Dad and shook him. "Dad, we gotta go. Wake up."

He mumbled in his sleep but didn't open his eyes. Jameson came up next to me and splashed something on Dad's face. It smelled like beer but did the job. Dad moved, his eyes half open.

"Willa?" he asked, his voice drowsy.

I took one side and Jameson the other, and together we hoisted him up to a standing position. He was dead weight, his feet not supporting him at all. Neither Jameson nor I wanted to stick around a second longer than we had to and started walking. Dad made half-hearted attempts at moving his feet, but it was mostly just Jameson carrying him outside.

He looked angrier than when he came inside. Double damn. I just hoped he wouldn't dump us on the side of the road somewhere.

We made it to his truck and leaned Dad up against the side. Jameson opened the door, and together we pushed and pulled Dad onto the back seat. He was lying on his side, feet hanging out of the truck, snoring softly.

I swallowed the bitter words that threatened to escape and instead lifted his feet onto the seat. I somehow buckled him in, and we managed to close the door.

"Get in," Jameson said, his voice betraying no emotion.

His jaw was clamped tight, the muscles working overtime. Since I had no intention of being on the receiving end of his wrath, I curled up as far away from him as the truck would allow and stayed quiet. We drove for twenty minutes without a sound, except for Dad's steady snore. It was beyond uncomfortable.

I was too nervous to sleep, the adrenaline still coursing through me in angry swirls. I'd really done it this time. I just hoped Jameson would honor his word and let me continue to work at the garage. I chanced a glance in his direction, and he didn't look any less angry than when he got in the truck. His hands gripped the steering wheel in a vice-like grip, and his whole body was strung tight.

I couldn't take the silence anymore and said, "Jameson, I—"

The truck suddenly swerved and came to a stop at the side of the road. Dust flew up all around us, and I was jerked forward. I braced my hand on the dash to avoid hitting my head and looked around frantically. Did we hit something?

Jameson opened his door and jumped out. I looked back to make sure Dad was okay, but he was still draped across the seat, unaffected by the sudden stop. Good thing I managed to get a seat belt around him.

Getting out of the truck seemed like the worst thing to do at this moment, but I did it anyway because Jameson was pacing back and forth like he was warming up for a marathon.

I approached him with halting steps, not sure I was doing the right thing. He seemed to want to be anywhere but near me. "Jameson."

He ignored me, so I tried again. I was anything if not persistent and apparently also suicidal. If I valued my life, I would have stayed in the truck and let him get on with his episode in peace.

"Jameson. What's going on?"

Turned out that was the worst thing I could have asked. He swung his angry gaze at me and stalked closer. I wasn't sure if this was where my flight instinct should have kicked in. I was almost 99 percent sure he wouldn't have helped carry Dad out of Greg's only to leave my body in a shallow grave in the desert.

"Let's talk about this," I said. Because that's what adults would do. Talk things through.

Jameson didn't stop, but instead he swooped me up —yes, swooped, because he didn't even slow down to pick me up—and pinned me to the passenger door. My feet were dangling off the ground, and I braced my arms on his shoulders.

Now, see, under normal circumstances I would have loved to be in this position. It was as close as I could get to him without taking my clothes off. It also brought me at eye level, and as mentioned before, I loved his eyes. I didn't have to look up for once. His strong arms held me securely against him, and I tightened my hold around his neck. His hold was firm, but not to the point of painful.

His nose was inches from mine, and his eyes spewed fire at me. "You want to know what's wrong?"

I nodded because apparently that's all my body would allow me to do at this stage.

"You nearly got yourself killed in there."

I squeezed his shoulders—and what shoulders they were—and tried to defuse the situation. "Now that's a bit dramatic. There would have been no killing. I'm positive that Greg didn't really want that much trouble. Maybe there would have been rape and torture, but definitely no killing."

His grip tightened to uncomfortable, and I stopped talking. Guess it wasn't as reassuring as it sounded in my head.

"Do you know what the hell it felt like to watch you bet yourself in place of your dad's debt?"

I shook my head. No more talking for me. My reassurance speech needed some work before I would whip that one out again.

And I realized in that moment that I was a little prick who waltzed in there only thinking of one thing. Dad. I didn't consider how Maisie or Stella would feel if they ever found out. I didn't consider Jameson because he growled at me whenever he was within hearing range.

I was the worst thing that ever happened to him. I had brought him nothing but trouble. And it was time I owned up to it. Wiggling in his tight grip, I squirmed until he set me back on the ground, and I put some distance between us.

"I'm so sorry for everything. I'm the worst thing that ever happened to you, and I'll do whatever I can to make it up to you. No more talking back. No more ordering things without permission. And I'll put in extra hours. I'll be the best receptionist in all of Humptulips."

"You're not getting it," he said, his voice was so low I had to stop my pacing to be able to hear him.

Instead of telling me what an absolute idiot I was, he closed the distance I managed to put between us and crushed his lips to mine. Holy donut, rainbows and fireworks.

His lips were soft and gentle, his touch turning my body to jelly. I'd be damned if I wouldn't take this chance. So I did the one thing that any sane person with half a brain would do and kissed him back. My tongue sneaked out and traced his lower lip. He opened up, and once our tongues met, my ovaries exploded.

I didn't know how long the kiss lasted, but that was a kiss for the history books. As I said, rainbows and fireworks. Near orgasm. From a kiss. I was ruined for any future kisses. Life would never be the same again. I didn't know a kiss could be so all-consuming.

Jameson sat me back on my feet, his hands holding me lightly by my waist. I was breathing hard, unable to meet his eyes.

"We should get going," I said, breathless, my voice raspy.

Jameson stepped back and let me go. We got in the truck in silence where Dad was still snoring, dead to the world, and pulled back onto the road. If my lips weren't still tingling, I would have thought the kiss never happened.

12

"You are not the worst thing that's ever happened to me." Jameson's voice startled me, and I jumped in my seat.

"What?" I asked, confused.

"You said you are the worst thing that's ever happened to me. It's not true."

Where should I start explaining to him how wrong he was? Let's go with the money angle first. I counted it off with my fingers. "My dad owes you a lot of money that he's unable to pay you back. I am a terrible receptionist. I managed to increase the debt instead of working it off. I make you angry, and your head looks like it's going to explode every time you're around me. You got sucked into an illegal poker game because of me. Take your pick."

I looked at his profile, hoping I wouldn't see his angry vein pulsing. God, he was gorgeous.

"You're putting a lot of importance on yourself. All of what you just said sounds like your dad screwed up and you tried to fix it. And I came to Vegas by choice; nobody made me."

He sounded almost happy. Why did he sound almost happy? I was one coffee machine away from ruining his life. "I'll do everything I can to pay back what my dad owes you while staying out of your way. It will be like I'm not even there."

"Well, see that's just not going to work for me."

Not going to work for him? NOT GOING TO WORK FOR HIM? At this stage, I wasn't sure if we were still talking about me working for him or something completely different. I got that he thought he liked me. But for how long? Until the next girl came walking past, flashing her tits at him?

I liked him. A lot. And I had no fucking idea what to do with all his attention focused on me. I watched with big eyes as he took his hand off the steering wheel and reached over. He pulled my hand off my lap and placed it on his thigh, his own hand on top.

What the ever-loving fuck was going on? "Um, Jameson, what are you doing?"

He stroked my hand with his thumb and answered, "Holding your hand. What does it look like I'm doing?"

"Okay. Why are you holding my hand?"

"Because I want to."

There was really nothing I had to say to that. I had just caused him to have possibly the worst day of his life, and his response was to hold my hand.

There was nothing I wanted more than to wrap myself around him at that moment, but I had to keep my shit together. As long as my dad owed him money, I was not going to go down that road. It was wrong.

I sighed deeply and tried to pull my hand back, but his fingers tightened, and he didn't let go. I gave up and tried reasoning with him instead. "Look, Jameson, you are a great guy, but—"

"Hell no. You are not giving me that speech. I know that you are just as affected as I am. I can feel your pulse speed up every time I touch you, and you were as much into that kiss tonight as I was."

I really couldn't deny anything he'd just said since that had been my exact reaction. But I could try and get him to see what a stupid idea it would be if we went any further with this. "It's just simple physical attraction. It will pass. Just give it a few days."

He lifted my hand and kissed my knuckles. And damn, did my knuckles like that. Loved it, to be precise. "Jameson, what are you doing?" My voice had gone all soft and sappy.

"Showing you how wrong you are." He pulled over at the side of the road again and turned the engine off. He undid his seat belt and shuffled closer on the big bench seat until he was as close as he could get. I was squeezed in tight between Jameson's muscular body and the door. He didn't give me time to freak out. Instead his lips touched mine gently and his arms engulfed me, making any escape impossible, but escape was the last thing on my mind at that moment. All I could think about was how good it felt to kiss him, and then my mind went blank.

My eyes stayed closed when he finally pulled back, and I whimpered at the loss.

"Willa, open your eyes."

I shook my head. I wasn't ready. And I wanted more.

His hand lightly stroked my cheek, and I leaned into his touch, savoring the moment.

"I told you there was more to it than physical attraction. Tell me again that I'm wrong."

His smug tone made my eyes snap open, and I

pushed on his chest to gain some distance. “This proves nothing.”

“We both know that’s not true.”

He got back behind the steering wheel and pulled out onto the empty road. Oh boy, it was going to be a long drive home.

When he took my hand again, I knew I was in trouble because I didn’t even try to move it.

13

"Come on, honey, don't be mad," Dad pleaded. He had done the unthinkable and shown up at my apartment. In the two years that I had lived there, he had visited exactly three times. Twice for Christmas and once to hide from a loan shark.

"Don't be mad? DON'T BE MAD? I had to drive to Vegas. And Greg was ready to make me his newest whore. I played poker for you." The thought of Greg made me shiver. The thought of poker made me angry.

"Honey."

"Don't." I put up my hand, refusing to let him inside. I wasn't sure how much longer I could hold the tears at bay, but this time I absolutely had to. We couldn't keep the endless cycle of destruction going. He screwed up, I came to bail him out, and he screwed up again.

"You went too far this time. You're lucky Jameson was there because there was no way I could have dragged you out of there myself."

"Jameson? Why was he there?"

Now that was a question I wanted the answer to as well. "Because I work for him and he offered to help?"

"Hang on a minute, you're working for Jameson?"

"As if you didn't know. How do you think your debt is being paid off?"

"I paid it off. Well, technically Des did."

"You what? When?" I couldn't believe what I was hearing.

Dad shifted from one foot to the other before answering, "Couple of weeks after the race, Des found out how much I owed. He paid Jameson."

My head was spinning, and I was confused. Why would he insist I continue to work for him if there was no more debt to pay off?

"So you don't owe him money anymore?"

"Not Jameson, no. I owe Des, but he doesn't mind. Said I could pay him back whenever."

"You're telling me that Des just had a huge chunk of money lying around?"

Dad reached out a hand to pull me to him. I stepped back, not ready to forgive and forget. He flinched at my rejection but dropped his arms. "Do you remember when Des invested in that old factory a few years back? The one near Drover's field?"

Of course I remembered. Everyone in town would. It was a huge scandal, the factory exploited its workers, then burned down under mysterious circumstances.

Des had inherited money from his late wife's parents. He was the only one named in the will and blew it all on the factory. At least that's what I thought. "What does that have to do with anything? Did he have money left?"

"He didn't lose it all and opened a trust fund for you so you could go to school. He kept another account for rainy days."

"Why didn't you ever tell me about this? I've been working my ass off to make ends meet and make sure all your bills are paid. The extra money would have come in handy."

Dad looked embarrassed and refused to meet my eyes. Fuck it all to hell, I knew a guilty look when I saw one. "Dad, what happened to the money?"

"It was a safe bet," Dad defended himself, and I knew there wouldn't be a cent left.

"You used the money Des gave you for me and gambled it away."

My hands were shaking, and my voice had gone up an octave or two. How could he? The last two years had been hell. I had no social life. Barely got any sleep. I worried about money every single day, and he had the means to make it all go away. But he didn't. Instead, he lost it all.

"I can't believe you."

"Willa, baby girl, it was a sure thing. I didn't think I could lose."

"But you did," I yelled at him, tears streaming down my face.

"Honey…," Dad whispered. I didn't hear what else he said as I stepped back and slammed the door in his face.

I sank to the floor and sat there, numb, tears still going strong. I knew Dad had a problem. He always liked to party and gamble. But only since Mom died did he stop caring about the people around him. Uncle Des would never see his money again. But he would have known that when he agreed to give it to his brother.

A ping on my phone ripped me out of my trance. I wiped my eyes with the backs of my hands and got up.

My phone was on the kitchen counter, angrily blinking at me, alerting me of the message I'd heard come in.

I cursed when I picked it up, first seeing Jameson's name on the screen and then the time. I remembered my shift at the garage, a job I didn't really have to do anymore. Then I also remembered that Jameson made me work for him for free. For weeks I had been coming in, thinking I was working off Dad's debt.

I clicked on the message and blinked hard at the tears forming in my eyes. The traitorous bastard had some nerve.

Jameson: *Come and find me when you get in.*

The sadness was quickly replaced with anger. And it was no longer directed at Dad but Jameson. I could handle anger, but sadness not so much. Mind made up too quickly for a good decision, I grabbed my keys, stuffed my phone in my back pocket and marched out of my apartment. Dad wasn't there anymore, much to my relief, and I sprinted down the stairs.

I didn't remember much of the short drive. Landon was talking to a customer when I pulled up outside the shop. He smiled at me and waved in greeting, but his expression dropped when he saw the look on my face. DEFCON 1 was about to happen. He said something to the customer and shook his hand before jogging over to me.

"Hey, Will, wait up."

"Not now, Landon."

"What's wrong, honeycakes?"

"Where is Jameson?" I hissed.

Landon took a step back. "Whoa, what crawled up your ass and died?"

"If you can't tell me where he is, then get out of my way."

He immediately took another step back. Fine, if he wanted to be a little bitch chicken, so be it. I'd find Jameson myself. There weren't many places he could be.

I stormed into the garage and looked around the bays. Mason waved at me with the wrench he was holding. "Willa, you have returned. Glad you brought my brother back in one piece too. Last time he went to Vegas, he came back with a black eye and a broken arm."

He might end up like that after all. "Have you seen him?"

"Yeah, he's helping Clay with the old transmission we got in yesterday. Thinks he might be able to put it in the Mustang."

Clay's bay was just two cars over, and since I was pretty much running, I made it there within a few seconds. I heard steps behind me, and a look over my shoulder confirmed that both Landon and Mason were following me, albeit at a safe distance.

I spotted Jameson's stupid sexy mop of hair bent over an engine. I shook my head to clear it and get back on track. Just had to remember the anger, not how good his ass looked in a pair of jeans.

"Jameson," I said, my voice low and barely controlled. My whole body was vibrating in anger. His head snapped up, and he smiled at me in greeting. Stupid cute smile and stupid gorgeous eyes.

With my hands on my hips, my chest pushed out and standing tall, I started yelling at him. Definitely wasn't making good decisions today. "You made me work for you even though Dad had already paid you back your money." Straight to the point was always my philosophy. I was also worried I'd lose my momentum and chicken out if I didn't say what I thought straight up.

Jameson wiped his hand on a dirty rag and faced me. "Willa, it's not what you think."

I huffed and puffed, and I wouldn't be surprised if there was steam coming out of my ears. "How is it not what I think? How do you even know what I think?"

He took a step closer but stopped when he saw my angry, squished face. "I know how bad this looks, but I would never make you work for free."

"How is it not making me work for free if I'm under the impression I'm working off my dad's debt, when in reality I'm working without getting paid while you already got the money he owed you back?" I was yelling, and everyone was staring. There was no coming back from this one.

"Fuck, you didn't," Mason said.

Clay elbowed him. "Shut up, Mason. I don't want to miss it when she punches him. It's going to be epic."

Jameson gave the finger to his brother and Clay. "Fuck off. Get back to work; I need to talk to Willa."

"No way."

"I'm staying."

"We're so watching this."

The guys responded and didn't move an inch.

I didn't care either way. "Nothing to say for once?" I spat at him, too far gone to see his approach through the red filter that seemed to have settled on my vision.

"I'm not discussing this with you in front of the boys. This is about us, nobody else."

"There is no us," I yelled, waving my arms around wildly, looking for something to throw at him. I spotted a piece of rubber on the floor and went to pick it up. I made it one step before I was lifted up and found myself hanging upside down. "Let me go, you lying jerkface."

"Not a chance," he said, patting my butt.

The guys watched us with wide grins, making no move to help me. "Why are you just standing there? Help me."

"You're in good hands, honeycakes," Landon said, and everyone scattered. Traitors.

If they thought they could just abandon me, they were sadly mistaken. There would be hell to pay as soon as I could get down from the far heights I was currently stuck on. I started pounding my hands across Jameson's back but soon realized what a bad idea that was when I made contact with his firm ass.

So I thought, to hell with it, stopped hitting him, and instead planted my hands firmly on his delectable behind.

"I thought you were mad at me," Jameson said, sounding entirely too amused.

"I am." My hands were too busy touching him, and my brain wasn't really functioning at the moment.

"Then why are you feeling me up?"

"You owe me."

He chuckled, and the vibrations went straight between my legs.

We made it up the stairs leading to his apartment in record time. I wish I was upright so I could enjoy this momentous occasion of being allowed into Jameson's inner sanctum. I pushed up to look around and nearly knocked myself out on the doorframe.

I caught a glimpse of a small but clean living room and a brand spanking new kitchen. Jameson pushed through a half-closed door at the end of the hall that seemed to be a bedroom. And judging by the clothes all over the floor, it was *his* bedroom.

I didn't have much time to process my findings when I was flung onto the bed and Jameson landed on top of me. He caught himself on his arms, so he didn't crush me. And since full-body contact with Jameson was like Christmas and Easter in one glorious moment, and even though I was still mad, I didn't mind our new arrangement at all.

"Let's talk," he said, his mouth only inches from mine.

I blinked at him and tried my best not to move my head and close the space between us. The smirk on his face told me he knew exactly what he was doing, and he knew he was doing it well.

"You lied to me."

"Technically, I didn't mention a few things. I didn't outright lie."

I narrowed my eyes at him. "Same thing. You made me think Dad owed you a lot of money."

He looked contrite and lowered his gaze, bringing his eyes in line with my boobs.

The silence between us grew but wasn't uncomfortable. He continued to stare at my chest, and I continued to stare at his perfect hair. Girls would kill for hair like his, thick and shiny. I was dying to touch it, and if he didn't move his head up soon, I wouldn't be able to stop my hands from reaching out.

There was no touching, but his body tightened against mine and he said, "I'm sorry I didn't tell you as soon as your dad came to see me. At first you were the perfect solution. I got a new receptionist and my money back at the same time. And then when you started working here…." He didn't finish his sentence but lifted his head and looked at me with such reverence I forgot to breathe.

"Then what?" I asked, my voice hushed.

"Then I liked having you around. You are a whiz in the office. The guys love you. The customers rave about you."

I never, not in a million years, thought Jameson would ever think I did a good job. "So this is really just a smart business decision."

He nodded. "The best I've ever made."

He was suspended above me for only a second before he closed the distance between us and softly placed a kiss on my mouth. His movements were slow, reverent, and I soaked up every touch, every caress. I was immobile, stunned. He traced light kisses along my jaw and neck, and I sighed at the sensations running through my body.

His lips met mine again, and he traced my lip with his tongue. It was too much, the sensations over-powering.

I didn't pull back but instead our slow kiss turned into a frenzied meeting of tongue and lips. There was no way I'd be stopping now, not when the only thing I wanted in that moment was to get closer.

One of his hands made their way underneath my shirt, and I arched into his touch. He blazed a hot trail up my body, making me squirm.

The kiss broke, and we were both breathing hard. He had lost his shirt at some point, and by the way I was clutching the fabric in my hand, it must have been me who had ripped it off. I released the shirt and placed my hands on his chest. I was tentative at first, but when he smiled a crooked smile at me and shuddered at the contact, I gained confidence.

I travelled lower, feeling each ridge and bump of his abs along the way. When my greedy fingers met his jeans, I stopped and looked at him, silently asking for permission. He nodded, and my hand roamed further, undoing his button and sliding inside. My eyes went wide when I felt him. The rumors were true, thank you blessed donut god.

He groaned when my hand squeezed him gently, and the low rumble sent tingles up my body. I didn't know it could be like this. He moved down, and my hand slipped out of his pants and back up his side to come to a stop at his arms.

I loved the definition and hardness, relished in this glorious moment where I got to touch him so freely. And touch him I did.

"Promise me you're not going to regret this," Jameson said, his breath hot on my belly.

There was no way I would be able to form a coherent sentence while he was kissing his way down my body, so I sighed instead.

He stopped, and I squeaked in protest. He looked up. "Willa, promise me."

I bit my lip and nodded. He didn't seem convinced at my half-assed nod. "I need to hear you say it."

My breath was still heavy, my blood rushing through my head, making it hard to think, let alone talk. "I promise," I whispered, my body aching to get his touch back. Blessed be all hot sex gods, the two words seemed to be enough for him to continue on his path.

And continue he did until he found his destination and his tongue invaded my hot center. He added a finger, and I nearly combusted. The man was skilled, but I would have expected nothing less. Practice makes perfect and all that.

It took me about three seconds to combust and see stars. Those fingers were magic, and his tongue needed a special place in heaven. I could be embarrassed about how quick I went off, but that would require my brain to function.

He kissed his way back up my body, leaving a blazing trail in his wake. A girl could get used to this.

When he kissed the spot behind my ear, I couldn't suppress the shiver and moan. That had never happened. I was addicted and desperate to feel him inside me.

"I need you." My voice didn't sound like it belonged to me, and my body seemed to have a mind of its own. Before I could make bad decisions and regret this day worse than I knew I already would, Jameson reached inside his nightstand. The crinkle of a foil paper told me he was being forever levelheaded and wondered how he could have such an effect on me while he seemed completely in control.

He pushed inside, slowly, and my body welcomed him with open legs. I pushed up to get closer, and Jameson stilled.

He was panting hard, and if the pinched brows and thin mouth were any indication, he didn't look like he was having as much fun as I was right now.

"Did I do something wrong?" I asked, the thought that he wasn't really into this hit me like a bucket of water.

He looked down, and his face softened immediately. "Nothing is wrong. You are perfect. This is perfect. And I want it to last, but I don't think I can. Not when you keep moving like that."

I grinned at him and moved again while I pulled him back and pressed my mouth to his. I felt his smile and took that as full steam ahead. Instead of him leading, I rolled him over until he was on his back and I was straddling his hips. I sat up, admiring the view, and licked my lips.

"You're really making this hard for me."

I wiggled my brows at him. "Good, because otherwise this wouldn't work."

He chuckled, and I felt the vibrations inside my body. When I started to move slowly up and down, he gripped my hips. He guided me, slow at first and then quicker and deeper. I didn't think it was possible, but my body exploded a second time, and Jameson was right behind me. My limbs refused to function any longer, and I collapsed on his chest.

My mind stilled, and I soaked it all in, savoring each breath I got to take on his glorious chest. I memorized every caress of his hand on my back, every little kiss he placed on my head, cheek, nose, and neck.

We stayed like that, neither one of us saying anything while Jameson continued his lazy strokes and I snuggled in as close as I could get. There was plenty of time for regret later. For now I was in a Jameson fog and happier than I ever remembered being.

Instead of trying to get rid of me like I expected, he gently placed me down next to him and went to the bathroom to clean up. I didn't know if I should stay or go but the question was answered for me when he came back and lifted me half on top of him, our limbs intertwined, and pulled a blanket over our bodies.

I guess I was taking a nap in the middle of the day.

14

I WOKE UP WITH A START. MY LIMBS SCREAMED IN protest when I tried to move. I didn't drink last night, but I was feeling sore. My brain finally caught up when I noticed an arm around my middle. Jameson was pressed up against my back, making a silent escape impossible.

It also reminded me about yesterday. And last night. But why was I still here? He was also known for kicking his hookups out the door as soon as the sun came up. The sun was up, yet here I was.

A glance at the digital clock on his nightstand confirmed it was nearly eight in the morning. Things promised to get awkward if he woke up and still found me in his bed. Maybe if I wiggled out from underneath him, he would never know that I spent the night.

After we finally made it back to the garage yesterday afternoon, I buried myself in work and ignored the guys who seemed to come into the office more than usual. They claimed they needed coffee. Or food from the kitchen. Or a mop, which I knew was a lie because I've never once seen them mop the floor.

And every time they walked past they made sure to

waggle their eyebrows at me. So I did what any sane woman would do, and for every creepy eye movement, I threw a pen at them.

Things got even weirder when Jameson came in at five and asked me what I wanted for dinner. I was so freaked out that I mumbled incoherently, and he understood that to mean pizza. Before I knew what was happening, I found myself sitting on his couch, watching a renovation show and eating pizza.

I must have passed out somewhere around the bathroom renovation because I was dreaming of giant sinks coming after me.

This brought me to my current dilemma of finding myself in Jameson's bed without any recollection of how I got there.

I held on to the edge of the mattress and tried to pull myself out from underneath him. His arm was holding on to me as if I were a six-inch sub, and no matter how hard I wiggled, he wasn't budging.

I would have to remove his death grip first. I released the mattress I had used to pull away and gripped his hand that immediately curled around mine. I lifted it off me, the strategy successful when he let go of my body.

What I didn't plan on was him now holding on to my hand. I moved out of his embrace an exact two millimeters before I started huffing at the effort. He was heavy and not moving. He was also holding my hand, which was now resting on my hip, making it hard to get anywhere unless I had the ability to dislocate my shoulder.

I sank back into the mattress, at a loss of what to do. My options at this stage were limited. If I was being honest with myself, I more than enjoyed nearly being crushed by Jameson. He was like a warm, safe, delicious-smelling cocoon. Initial panic at waking up in his bed over, I decided to allow myself a few more minutes before I faced reality. My body sagged back against his, and I prayed he would stay asleep.

"That's better," he muttered into my ear, and I went tense all over again. That bastard was awake. He pulled me impossibly closer and kissed my head. "Stop wiggling."

"I need to go," I forced out, glad I wasn't stuttering.

"It's Sunday." As if that explained everything.

"I have to water my plants."

"Do it later."

Of course, I didn't shut up. Sometimes I really wasn't sure how I made it through life. "They are on a watering schedule. The next round is due at eleven." Oh, please someone stop me from talking.

Jameson must have thought the same because I found myself on my back, Jameson hovering above me. "Stop panicking."

"I'm not panicking."

"You are the queen of panic. And I can tell by your crazy eyes that you are one eye roll away from breaking out into a mad cackle."

"I don't cackle."

"Babe."

My eyes stopped rolling, and instead I stared straight at Jameson. He had called me babe. I'd never been anyone's babe. I bit my lip to stop myself from saying anything. Must. Not. Ruin. The. Moment. A moment I would remember until I was lying cold and dead in my grave.

He kissed my nose. My nose! And then the corner of my mouth. Why hadn't he kicked me out yet?

"Stay. Please." His plea was followed by another kiss, this time on my neck. I shivered. The bulge on my stomach told me that he was happy to see me. Not sure my vagina could handle it.

He placed a gentle kiss on my mouth and looked at me. All I could do was stare. Things like this didn't happen to me. I had the worst luck out of anyone I knew. Not once had I won anything, got a green light when I needed it, or caught the full coffee cup before it hit the floor. But all that seemed insignificant if it meant Jameson continued to look at me like he did at this moment. With reverence. Like I was precious to him.

"Spend the day with me."

His request threw me for a loop. This version of Jameson was dangerous. It was making me have warm and fuzzy feelings. I wanted to throw my arms around his neck and shout yes. But that would be impossible, not only because my arms were pinned to my side but also because then he'd realize what a nutcase I really was.

I was helpless to do anything but put a big goofy smile on my face and nod like a bobble head. His face lit up with an adorable grin, and he leaned down to kiss my lips. Once. Twice. Featherlight kisses that made me starved for more. Instead of deepening the kiss, he sat up.

I whimpered at the loss of his body but forgot all about it as soon as he smiled his crooked smile at me. He took my hand and helped me up until I was perched on the side of the bed, sheet in a death grip, a naked Jameson in front of me.

"Let's shower," he said and winked at me. There was no way I was getting in the shower with him. My body wasn't perfect, not by a long shot, and I had indulged in cupcakes way more than was healthy for my butt lately. Especially since he looked like a fucking Greek god. And, well, I did not. Look like a Greek goddess that is.

The point being, I was so not getting out of bed until he was safely tucked away in the bathroom.

"You can shower first," I said, not looking at him, hoping he'd get the hint.

I should have known better than to think I'd get away with hiding. He tugged on the sheet I had wrapped myself in. I clutched it tighter. He took my arm to help me up; I shuffled back.

He must have thought it was time to bring out the big guns because he smiled his damn irresistible smile at me. "It's a big shower. There's room for two."

I lowered my head to avoid his stupid sexy smile and to tell him that I was fine and he could go ahead and shower when my eyes got stuck along the way. He was naked, and his body was a work of perfection. And his cock was obviously excited to see me. Oh my. I licked my lips and swallowed. I never thought I'd say this, but there wasn't a part of his body that wasn't attractive.

"I…," I started but wasn't sure anymore what I wanted to say. All I could think was if I leaned forward a little, I could lick him. Just one little lick. Just to taste him.

He used my distraction against me, and the sheet was ripped away and I found myself lifted up into the air.

"What are you doing?" I shrieked, holding on for dear life.

He carried me into the shower bridal style and sat me down on the counter next to the sink. "Don't move."

"But I can't take a shower with you," I sputtered.

He turned the water on and came back. His hands

were on either side of my hips, making an escape once again impossible. "We both need a shower. Let's save water and take it together."

He lifted me up again and placed me in the shower. I stood on shaky legs, something that seemed to happen a lot around him, and stepped under the spray. The warm water felt great on my sore muscles, and his showerhead was huge. There would be no taking turns, because we could both fit underneath the spray. If we stood close. Jameson didn't seem to have a problem with that and pulled me close, his hands travelling up and down my body. I sank into him and tilted my head under the spray.

My self-consciousness evaporated as soon as he started shampooing my hair and then washing my body. He occasionally stopped and told me how beautiful I was. He also stopped to place kisses all over my body.

It was safe to say I was a goner. Done. Melted. A puddle. He was too much. He lingered on my breasts, kissing and sucking each one until I was panting. He sent me over the edge when he slipped his finger inside me. It was like he flipped a switch and I went off.

He held me to him, his hands lazily trailing up and down my back, giving me a chance to get my breathing under control.

"My turn," I declared with a smirk on my face. He handed me the soap and stood in front of me, watching my every move.

I wouldn't miss this opportunity to explore every inch that was Jameson Drake. I had the chance to get my hands on him, and I would take it. I started on his chest and made a soapy trail down to his abs, feeling every ridge along the way. I circled around his arousal, teasing him. Once my hand closed around his shaft, he groaned, and I loved the effect I had on him. My hands weren't enough, and I knelt down, licking the tip. His hands went into my hair. "Fuck."

Oh yes, that was the plan. It was also all the invitation I needed, and I took him into my mouth. He was too big and long to fit fully, but whatever I couldn't fit I covered with my hand. I circled my tongue around the tip, tasting him.

I was just getting started, but Jameson had other ideas. His thigh muscles tightened, and he growled, "Willa." Always the gentleman, he gave me a chance to pull away, but I didn't want to. I wanted to taste him, something I never had an interest in before. But Jameson seemed to break down all my walls and restraints. He came inside my mouth, and I swallowed every last bit.

He helped me back up and kissed me, his breathing still hard, his kiss bruising. "What are you doing to me?" he asked against my mouth.

"I don't know, but can we do it again?" I answered, feeling too good to care that I wasn't wearing a stitch of clothing or that I just went all hussy on him. He made me feel comfortable, cherished, and wanted.

We got out and dried off before getting dressed. Jameson held my hand on the way to his truck and helped me in. He placed a kiss on my lips before closing the door. A girl could get used to this. And I definitely wasn't going to freak out.

15

I TOTALLY FREAKED OUT. I OVERANALYZED EVERY LITTLE movement, gesture, and word coming from Jameson. By the time we made it to the diner, I was a mess. There was no way I could eat lunch. He touched me every chance he got, held my hand, and kissed my cheek. He was attentive. He was the perfect date.

And I was not. First I spilled my soda on his lap. Then I spewed bits of food on his shirt when he asked me if I was ready to go home so he could have his dessert.

I should quit while I wasn't completely humiliated and just go home. But Jameson didn't seem to care about the level of crazy I had apparently reached. He carried on as if nothing had happened, wet stain on his jeans and all.

And I liked him more each time he winked at me or made a joke about his wet crotch. We were just finishing up when a busty blonde sauntered up to our table, her focus entirely on Jameson. He was like a homing beacon. It was fascinating to watch. I also felt a pang of something foreign in my chest, and the feeling was not welcome. It felt especially nasty when he got out of his side of the booth and greeted her with a kiss on the cheek.

"Lu-Anne."

I could forgive him for greeting her since I was a grown up and all, but what I couldn't forgive was the way she touched him. Hands on his chest, a chest that I had licked not too long ago. And the way she was standing entirely too close didn't exactly stop the murderous thoughts running through my head.

"You forgot this at my place," she purred and pulled a ball cap out of her bag.

"I was wondering where I left that," Jameson replied and took the cap from her. "Thanks for dropping it off."

"Mason told me you'd be here."

"Not hard to figure out since I come here every Sunday."

He turned away from her to get back into his seat, but she stopped him by putting a hand on his arm and pressing her ample chest to his side. "I'm free tonight," she whispered, loud enough for me to hear and grind my teeth. Why did I ever think I would have a chance against the pussy brigade that was following him around everywhere?

"I'm here with someone." Jameson nodded his head toward me, and pouty mouth turned her heaving breasts my way. Wowza, it would require an army to contain those monsters. A closer inspection—because who wouldn't stare if they were thrust in your face—revealed that she didn't seem to believe in bras. I tore my gaze away and met her eyes. She was sneering at me, and I couldn't say I was smiling at her.

"Come over later. I'll be home," she said while looking at me.

Jameson sat back down and took my hand. "I'm spending the day with Willa." *Ha, in your face, balloon skank.*

"Call me," she said, still not getting the message, but at least she finally left.

I pulled my hand out of Jameson's grip and leaned back. I may have pouted, but who could blame me? I just saw firsthand what I was up against, and it wasn't a pretty sight. Jameson seemed unfazed.

"Sorry about that." And that was it. That's all he had to say on the matter. Case closed. He was so clueless. As if I would be happy to just move on. I once made Maisie apologize for a whole week for forgetting to pick me up on her way to school. I could hold a mean grudge.

He left money on the table and got up. "What do you want to do for the rest of the day?"

"Jameson—" I started, but he put his hand on my mouth.

"Oh no, you don't. Lu-Anne was a mistake that I have no intention of repeating. Stop freaking out. Now I'm going to ask you again. What do you want to do today?"

Oh boy, he was better than I thought. Damn it all to hell, it would be too easy to just give in, but I couldn't. And there was the point where I was incredibly stubborn. "I think we shouldn't make this whole thing more complicated than it really is. I might not be working for you anymore, but we all know this isn't going anywhere. Cut our losses while it won't hurt any feelings, I say."

He crowded me against the table and took my face in his hands. "Fuck no. I've wanted this for years. I'm not just standing back and watching you talk yourself out of giving us a chance."

I had absolutely no response to that. What in the ever-loving fuck did he mean that he wanted this for years? He didn't even know me a couple of weeks ago. I was about to tell him just that when he picked me up and threw me over his shoulder. My face went red, partly from hanging upside down, partly from the embarrassment of everyone looking at us. Everyone in Humptulips would know that we'd done the deed. I was never gladder for Maisie and Stella's absence than at this moment. They would give me hell for going near Jameson if they knew.

"You can't just end every argument by throwing me over your shoulder, you caveman. It doesn't work that way." I slapped his firm butt. "Hey, are you listening to me?"

"Nope. There is nothing to discuss. And we didn't have an argument. You were chickening out again. So I'm making this decision for us. We are going back to my apartment, where you'll stay until tomorrow morning."

"Excuse me?" My concern gave way to anger. "What the fuck gives you the right to make a decision like that for me? What if I have to go home? What if I left my stove on?"

"You don't cook."

He put me down in front of his truck, caging me in with his big body while opening the door. I was once again lifted into the seat. He even locked the door after he closed it. As if I didn't know how to unlock a door. I fumbled for the handle but couldn't find the unlock button. Damn truck didn't have a lock on the door. Turned out I didn't know how to open a goddamn door after all.

Jameson got in and grinned at me. "You tried to get

out but couldn't unlock the door, didn't you?" The smug bastard. I crossed my arms and leaned back in my seat.

He leaned over, and I held my breath. His face was inches from mine, and I fought the urge to close the distance. I liked his kisses. A lot. And I wanted him to kiss me again. Often. But right then I was mad at him.

Reading my mood, he reached around me to get the seat belt out and buckled me in. With one last wink in my direction, he sat back in his seat and pulled out of the parking lot.

Once he somehow maneuvered me back into his apartment, I was stunned. What I didn't expect Jameson to do was to watch a movie with me. Or to cuddle on the couch. Or to cook me dinner. I also didn't think he'd want me to stay the night again, which I wasn't prepared for since I didn't bring a change of clothes. I could only turn my underwear inside out so many times.

Jameson ignored my protest and instead gave me one of his shirts and boxers to sleep in. Not that I put up much of a fight. It was one of the best days I'd ever had. It was perfection, because I got to spend it with Jameson.

When we eventually went to bed, I was ready to tear my hair out. All I wanted was for him to make a move. Instead he tucked me in and spooned me. Now, any other time I would have been over the moon. But I was on fire from all his little touches and caresses throughout the day. Spooning was just not going to do it for me.

I turned around so we were nose to nose, mouth to mouth.

"Hey," I said. Lame, I know, but my brain tended to shut down every time I was close to him.

He grinned at me. "Can't sleep?"

That bastard. He knew exactly what he was doing to me. Two could play that game.

"I'm fine. Just wanted to turn around."

I felt his erection press against my thigh and blinked at him innocently. His grin faltered, and he pulled me closer. I kissed his cheek and closed my eyes. "Okay, goodnight."

I heard a groan, and then I found myself flat on my back, pinned down by the Neanderthal. "I don't think so," he growled.

"Changed your mind?"

"My mind was always made up. Nothing to change."

"Then why the spooning?"

"I wanted to make sure you knew that I don't just want one thing from you. I like having you close."

Now, that went straight to places that didn't need any more stimulation. And the night went places I couldn't ever seem to get enough of. Definitely one of my favorite days.

When my alarm rang, I'd had a grand total of two hours of sleep. I was tired but happier than I ever remember being.

"What is that?" Jameson grumbled into my hair.

"My alarm. Go back to sleep."

"Why would you set your alarm for—" He looked at his nightstand and frowned. "—fucking three in the morning?"

"I have to go to work."

"You go to work at three?"

"Have to be there by four, and I'm slow in the morning. Usually it takes me about four hits of the snooze button, two cups of coffee, and a cold shower to be awake enough to drive."

Jameson seemed wide awake now. "How often do you get up this early?"

"I work at the bakery Monday to Friday, sometimes on Saturdays if Rayna needs me."

His face turned dark, and he frowned at me. "Are you telling me that you've been working at the bakery in the morning and then coming to the garage?"

I moved out of his arms and detangled my legs from his. "Yes?" It sounded more like a question, but I wasn't sure why he was suddenly so angry.

"You've been working for me for weeks."

"Yes?"

"Don't you also work at the Donut Hole?"

"Some nights."

"What the fuck, Willa?" He looked ready to burst a blood vessel.

I scrambled out of bed, glad I put on a shirt and underwear before I fell asleep. "I should go. I don't want to be late."

"You're always late. And you shouldn't be working three jobs."

It was my turn to glare at him, but he didn't seem affected in the least. He also didn't seem to want to let this conversation die the slow and awkward death it deserved.

I scrambled for my jeans that I had thrown on the floor the night before. "What difference does it make? You blackmailed me into working for you. I didn't think you'd care that I already had two jobs."

Finally I spotted my jeans and stepped into them. They were about halfway up my legs when Jameson appeared next to me. I hopped up and down to speed up the process and get out of there. I didn't understand why he was upset. I told him I didn't want to work for him from the start. This should not be breaking news.

His face was serious. Way too serious for three in the morning. "Willa, I would have never made you work for me full time if I'd known." His anger morphed into regret.

I avoided looking at him and turned back to wrestling with my clothes. "All good. No hard feelings, especially now that I don't work for you anymore." I managed to get the jeans over my butt and hold my breath to close the button. After another short struggle with my shirt, I was fully dressed. For some reason it made me feel much more confident, and I turned to face a hovering Jameson.

"I really do need to go."

He stepped closer and put his arms around me. I automatically sank into him, putting my hands on his smooth chest that I would never get enough of touching.

He leaned his head down, pressing his cheek against mine. "Would you still come back for a few hours each week? The office has never been so organized, and the new software you bought is amazing. Cuts our paperwork in half."

Right, I forgot I purchased software without getting him to approve it first. Probably should have asked for permission, but at the time it seemed like a great way to piss him off.

"I'll think about it."

He leaned down and kissed me, his mouth now familiar and something I didn't think I ever wanted to live without again. He pulled back after one last kiss to my cheek. "It will be easy money. And I'll actually be paying you this time, plus the money I owe you, of course."

He must have forgotten about the coffee machine, but who was I to remind him?

With one last glance over my shoulder—because let's be honest, who wouldn't look until the last minute when faced with a half-naked Jameson?—I left his apartment.

16

"You're late," Rayna greeted me when I was stumbling through the door of Sweet Dreams' kitchen.

I was breathless from running all the way from my car. All I could get out between breaths was, "Puppy."

She scoffed at my response but knew better than anyone that I was most likely telling the truth. I didn't mess around when it came to animals, and I had a slight obsession with puppies. Mrs. Winters, the neighbor who lived below me, just got a new puppy, and it was the cutest thing I had ever seen. When I ran into her on my way out of my apartment after running home to change my clothes, there was no way I could not stop and let the fluffy white and black ball of fur jump all over me.

Hence, why I was late.

Rayna threw my apron at me like she did every morning, which I never caught. I picked it up from the floor and got my marching orders for the day.

"New flour delivery arrived yesterday, so we're good to go for the Stevens' wedding. I'm on cupcakes; you make the cake. They want stupid little red bowties and hearts, which means I'm out. They've already picked their cake toppers." She threw a spatula my way, which landed on the counter. She never stopped throwing shit at me. Shit that so far I hadn't caught once. She wrinkled her nose, ignoring my terrible catching skills, and continued her tirade. "Stupid ridiculous cake topper."

"I'm on it. Did they decide if they wanted the red velvet or Belgian chocolate?"

"Both."

The answer I dreaded the most. Why couldn't people just make up their minds? It was easy. Pick one or the other. Now I had to get two different batches ready and decide which layer was which.

I knew it would be pointless to moan since Rayna would only take that as her God-given right to give me more work to shut me up.

"You look like death," she said, eyeing my wonky ponytail and stained T-shirt.

I poked my tongue out at her. "And you look like you just stepped out from underneath a rainbow and bathed in glittery unicorn farts."

Rayna threw a piece of dough that smacked me square in the face. "It's the new shampoo. Does wonders for my hair."

I removed the dough from my cheek, and we settled into work, silently passing ingredients back and forth. The familiarity of the tasks and working with Rayna finally calmed me down enough to sort through my head. Was I supposed to call Jameson? Would he want me to? Did I want to call him?

"Are you trying to make butter?" Rayna interrupted me.

"Butter? No, I—" One look at the bowl confirmed I had indeed been whisking the cream long enough to make butter.

"Honey, what's going on with you? You never screw up a cake. You are good at it. If I didn't know better, I'd say you're almost as good as me, but you're way off your game today." She looked at the cake with a wince, and I followed her gaze. Fuck me sideways. That was definitely not white bows. And the chocolate was melting, making the frosting look like someone licked it. I must have forgotten to add the pudding mix.

"Shit, shit, shit. I'll fix it. Don't worry, you'll have the cake on time. Promise."

Rayna raised her brows but didn't tell me that it was nearly impossible to fix what I had screwed up in the short time I had left. "You have two hours. Then I'll have to deliver everything to the Boathouse."

Now this was huge news. Under no circumstances could I screw this up for her. The Boathouse was the most exclusive wedding venue we had in town. It was also incredibly expensive. If you got a catering gig there you were set for life, not only because it would be worth a lot of money but because the exposure was priceless.

"The Boathouse? Are you serious? Rayna, that's amazing. Who did you bribe to pull that off?"

Rayna laughed and batted her long eyelashes. "It's all thanks to my incredible talent."

And I believed it because she really was the cake whisperer. "I'm going to get this cake done. And it's going to be the best cake I've ever made. I won't let you down."

And I wouldn't because I could never repay Rayna for all she had done for me over the years. The countless nights she sat up with me after Mom died when I suffered from night terrors. All the times she helped me with my homework. Let me stay with her because Dad disappeared and I was too scared to stay at the trailer by myself. Uncle Des was still living in one of the nicer parts of Humptulips at that time. And his wife couldn't stand me, so I never asked for his help. The feeling was mutual.

She squeezed my arm. "I know you won't, sweetheart. I'll drop everything else off and then I can give you a hand. Back soon."

Rayna rolled out the trolley with all the cupcakes to pack it into the van she bought last winter. After too many melted deliveries, she finally caved and instead of carting around a million cooler boxes, she bought a van with built-in cooling. It was freezing cold, as I had found out a few weeks back when I had the task of staying in the back and holding on to the massive cake we made.

It didn't take long for scrapes and dents to mysteriously appear on the chassis. Rayna vehemently denied any involvement, but she was a terrible driver. It was a miracle her cakes made it in one piece.

"Remember red means stop," I said to her retreating back.

She waved her hand without turning around, and if I didn't know better I would have thought her middle finger was slightly extended. I got back to mixing the icing, this time using the right ingredients. I had already made up the roses and rings that were supposed to go all over the cake. I was going to get this done, and Rayna would kick this wedding's ass.

And I did it. After two burnt fingers thanks to the melted chocolate, nearly cutting off part of my hand, and pouring the cream all over myself, I did it. The cake was done, and it looked pretty awesome. Just in time to witness my greatness, I heard the back door open. Rayna was going to love this. "I kick some serious cake ass, Rayna. It's a masterpiece. And I want a pay rise."

"You're already getting one in your other job."

I froze midway through my victory dance, which included my signature move, the robot, and turned around. There stood Jameson in all his Jameson glory, wearing a tight black T-shirt with the Drake Garage logo printed on the front. His jeans fit entirely too well, and I fought the urge to hide under the counter. There were only three people who had ever seen my dance, and I had no intention of extending that circle.

"Jameson. What are you doing here?" I was out of breath from jumping around the kitchen.

"Can't I just visit my girl?"

"Your girl?"

He grinned and stepped closer. For every step he took, I took one myself, but in the opposite direction. The kitchen wasn't very big, and my ass soon made contact with the counter. Jameson kept going until his shoes met mine. His arms went on each side of my body, caging me in.

"I tried to call you."

Fucksticks, my phone. I hadn't seen it since last night, so it was very likely still at his place. "Don't have my phone," I pointed out unnecessarily.

"Figured, since you didn't answer. Thought I'd check on you to make sure everything's okay and bring you this." He held out my phone. "Found it on the bed." At that he winked at me.

I took the phone, careful not to touch him, because touching led to kissing. And kissing led to—nothing. Absolutely nothing. Because we were in a kitchen. At my place of work. "I'm in one piece, no limbs missing."

How was I always feeling like a schoolgirl with a crush whenever he was around? I tried slipping out under his arms, but he anticipated my move, and I found myself pressed to his front, his arms now around me. And boy did I like it.

He lifted me up and sat me on the counter. "Better make sure of your well-being myself."

I felt my legs being pushed apart, and Jameson stepped in the gap.

He pressed his lips lightly to my forehead. "Looks good to me." Followed up by a kiss to my nose. "Perky as ever." And then my cheeks. "Soft as always." The corner of my mouth was next. "Addictive." At the same time his hands slipped underneath my shirt, lightly tracing a line on my skin. "Life altering."

A brush of his mouth over mine, and I was a goner. My hands sank into his hair, and I returned his kiss with a desperation that scared me. My legs went around him like they were dying to all along, and he was finally as close as he could get. Right where I wanted him.

"I guess you managed to finish the cake and started the party without me."

Rayna's laughter spurred me into action. I pushed a startled Jameson back and jumped off the counter. His shirt was covered in cream and chocolate, and his hair was sticking up.

I knew I definitely didn't look any better if the strands of hair hanging around my face and the shirt that was still halfway up my torso were anything to go by. Before I got a chance to stutter my way out of this, Jameson put one of his trademark smirks on his face and held out his hand. "You must be Rayna. So nice to meet you. I'm Jameson."

She shook his hand, gaping like a fish. There goes another one. Unlike every other female, myself included, Rayna recovered quickly. "Make yourself useful and help us carry that monstrosity out to the car."

She pointed at the cake, and without waiting for a reply, she was out the door.

"This the one?" he pointed in front of him but not before placing a kiss on my cheek.

"The one and only. I usually just push it onto the trolley and then wheel it out."

He nodded, and together we slowly pushed the cake onto the trolley.

"You usually do this by yourself?" he asked.

I shook my head and followed him out the door. "Nah, Rayna helps me. Or more accurately, I help her."

Jameson pushed the cake next to the open van and lifted it inside without waiting for me to give him a hand. Nice.

Rayna winked at me behind Jameson's back. I grinned back at her, because really, what else was there to do?

"Thanks, Jameson. I got it from here." She turned to me. "Thanks for your help today, honey. Go home and make me proud. Just not a great aunt yet."

I turned beet red and narrowed my eyes at her. "Rayna," I hissed through clenched teeth. She was gone before I could yell at her.

"Hungry?" Jameson asked.

"Always."

"Let's get some breakfast."

"Together?"

He took my hand and pulled me along. "I hope that was a rhetorical question. Come on, I haven't eaten yet."

And that's how I found myself next to Jameson, eating grilled egg and bacon sandwiches for the second morning in a row.

I just finished the last sip of my coffee and debated

the wisdom of having another cup, which would bring my total up to five for today, when Jameson nudged my thigh with his. "So have you thought about coming back to work for me? Maybe a few days a week?" I opened my mouth to tell him no, and he held up his hands to stop me. "Just for a few hours."

I thought about it. The money he offered was great, and I could really use it. Next semester was going to be intense since I was taking extra classes so I could finish earlier. I really shouldn't say no to the added income.

"Three days and no more than four hours at a time."

"Four days and no more than three hours at a time."

"That's an extra day that I'd have to come in. Three days and maybe I can be persuaded to go up to five hours."

He studied me, and seemingly satisfied with what he saw, he put an arm around me, leaning in close. "And what could I do to persuade you to stay five hours?"

I pursed my lips and tapped my cheek with my finger. "Good question. What have you got?"

He kissed me sweetly on my mouth, keeping it all PG, much to my disappointment.

"Free breakfast."

I grinned at him. "A girl's gotta eat. What else?"

He kissed me again, and once again it was much too chaste and over too quickly. "Frequent sleepovers."

I nodded. "A girl's gotta sleep."

His next kiss was more heated, and I felt my breathing speed up. "Free mechanical services."

"A girl's gotta keep her car working."

He went in for the kill and kissed me again, this time his tongue traced my bottom lip, and I opened instantly. He swooped in, and I sighed into his mouth. Finally.

He stopped as quick as he had started and looked at me. "Do we have a deal?"

I nodded. "How could I say no to all that." My eyes swept up and down his body, and we both knew I wasn't talking about his free breakfast.

"Let's go to the garage. The boys will be excited to have you back."

"Just the boys?"

He nudged me to get up and shuffled out of the booth after me. "Maybe me too. But that all depends if you can show me how to use the accounting software you installed. Might be good if you wrote down all the passwords too, just so I can access my own computer."

I shook my head and followed him out the door, marveling at the ease in which he took my hand like he'd done it a million times before. "You didn't have to offer me my job back to get me to give you the passwords or show you how the software works."

"I know. And that's definitely not why I did it."

He helped me into his truck, and we drove the short distance to the garage. He never once let go of my hand.

It was like I'd never left. As soon as we arrived, Landon hugged me tight and complained about the lack of cupcakes. Mason winked at me when I passed his bay, and Clay nodded his head at me the same way he'd done so many times before. I had to admit that I would have missed the shit out of these guys if I had stuck to my guns and quit.

Jameson disappeared as soon as he was satisfied I was back in my office chair and wouldn't go anywhere.

Another great thing about continuing to work at Drake's was unlimited access to the coffee machine. And that's where I was when Landon came in, catching me having a little one on one time with the magical device.

"Oh how I've missed you, you little piece of awesomeness. Let momma make herself a golden drink of heaven," I said.

"Good to see you still worship the coffee gods. You're also the only person who knows how to work the machine so the coffee is actually drinkable." He sat down on one of the kitchen chairs around the table and put his feet up. "You gonna take pity on me and make me a cup as well?"

"Of course." I hid my grin and grabbed another cup. He was making this too easy. The machine was simple to use; all you had to do was press a few buttons. No idea how the guys couldn't figure it out. I even steamed the milk for him, but only to hide the blue food die I slipped into his cup. His mouth would be stained for at least a day. Payback was a bitch.

I had to work hard to suppress the giggles wanting to burst out and stuffed an old bagel in my mouth that I found in the fridge to shut myself up.

"So you finally got laid, huh?" Landon said in between sips.

I stopped chewing my dry bagel and shot him a glare. After a sip of my own coffee, I managed to swallow the sawdust in my mouth and respond. "What makes you say that? Can't a girl just be happy because it's a nice day and she's with her friends?"

Landon got up and picked his cup up off the bench while I smothered my bagel in cream cheese. "Sure you can. But I know that you spent ages in Jameson's apartment after he dragged you off. And seeing as you two are obviously still talking, I'd say he finally got in your pants."

"What do you mean finally?"

He winked at me and showed his dimple. "You've got something in your teeth." With that last parting comment, he disappeared out the door, and I raced to the bathroom to remove the piece of bagel that was lodged in my teeth.

The second I looked in the mirror and opened my mouth, I let out a shriek to rival all shrieks. That jerkoff farthead. My mouth was blue. He managed to switch our cups without me noticing. Damn you, bagel, you lured me in, distracted me with your sawdust consistency, and let him mess with me again.

I stared at my reflection in the mirror and balled my fists. "Landon needs to die," I said to blue-mouthed me. I had people to kill and a mouth to wash out.

17

I WAS RUNNING OUT TO THE GARAGE FLOOR, COMING slightly unhinged.

"Where's the fire?" Mason asked, when I stumbled over a wrench he had left on the floor.

"No fire. Where's Landon?"

His eyes went wide, and he started chuckling.

When I yelled at him, "What?" he started laughing so hard his face turned red. I pushed him out of the way.

"Not a word." The threat went unanswered, and he started singing the song, "Blue." If I hadn't already set my sights on Landon, I would have stopped and taken the time to inflict some hurt on Mason.

I walked to Landon's bay but was stopped by a big hand snaking around my waist and lifting me up. I struggled against the tight hold and kicked out my feet. "Let me go. This doesn't concern you."

A chuckle sounded too close to my ear to be ignored. Jameson's warm breath fanned across my cheek, and I stilled in his arms. "Let's take this back to the office."

"But I need to talk to Landon." My weak protest

died a quick death when he ignored me and carried me into the office, much to the amusement of the whole workshop. Traitors.

Once in the office, Jameson sat me on the desk and moved in front of me to thwart my escape attempts. "I'm guessing the reason why your mouth is blue is Landon."

"You guessed correctly," I mumbled, avoiding opening my mouth.

"What did you do?"

"What did I do? Why do you immediately think this is my fault? My mouth is blue, not his."

He didn't respond, but his face said it all. He didn't believe a word. I huffed out a breath, annoyed that he knew exactly whose fault it was my mouth was blue. I needed to work on my poker face.

"Fine. I put the food dye in his coffee, and he must have switched our cups when I wasn't looking." I avoided his eyes and stared at his lips instead, which turned out wasn't the greatest idea I ever had since it made me want to kiss him. But I decided that I was mad at him for not defending me, so there would be no kissing in his future.

"There is mouthwash in the bathroom. Not sure if that will help, but it's worth a try." He stepped back to let me off the desk, and I stormed past him without a second glance. "Oh, and, Willa, you should know that Landon never loses."

"We'll see about that."

The mouthwash didn't help much. When I usually got food dye on my skin at the bakery, I used lemon or baby wipes to get rid of it. Of course, neither was anywhere to be found in the office.

I dumped the coffee in the sink and made myself a

new cup. Time to regroup and figure out how to make Landon pay.

My phone vibrated on the counter where I dropped it in my rush to get to Landon. I didn't recognize the number but picked it up anyway. Could be Dad. "Hello?"

"Willa. I believe your dad has a debt to me that he is unable to pay."

Oh, for all that is holy, what the fuck had he done now? "Who the hell are you?" I was as tight as a bowstring.

"My name is Jacob. And that's no way to talk to the person holding Garret Montgomery's life in his hands."

A gasp escaped me before I could stop it, and I lowered the phone. My knees gave out, and I sank to the floor right where I stood in the middle of the kitchen. The floor was disgusting, covered in grease and green fluid, but I didn't care.

"Where is he?" My voice was loud, too loud. I had to get my shit together or risk pissing off the guy on the other end of the line more than I already had. "What did you do to him?" I added with much less force; this time my voice was pleading. Also not a good thing. Show no weakness and all that.

"Nothing yet. And his future well-being depends on you."

"Tell me what to do. I'll do anything." Wrong thing to say again. Hearing that Dad had gotten himself into trouble again so soon had thrown me so far off course, I didn't know if I would be able to walk in a straight line any time soon.

"I know you will. You and I have a deal to make."

"What kind of deal?"

"The one where I get my money."

"What do you want me to do?"

"Meet me. I'll text you directions."

I was so screwed. Surprisingly, I still hadn't won the lottery or inherited a fuckload of money.

"I will but can I talk to—"

The bastard hung up on me, but what did I expect? I tried calling Dad, but unsurprisingly he didn't pick up his phone. I left him a message to call me. Des was next. "Killa. What's a-shakin' little bacon?"

"Have you seen Dad today?"

"I think he's still sleeping. Last I saw of him was last night when he came home. Hasn't left his trailer since."

If that was true, my life would have just improved significantly.

"Can you please go and check?"

"Everything okay?"

"I'm fine, everything's fine. Just want to make sure Dad's doing all right."

"Are you still not talking to him?"

Des's voice sounded accusing, and I didn't like it. I wasn't the one in the wrong. My voice got defensive. "He made me drive all the way to Vegas because he gambled away everything but the clothes on his back. Now ask me again if I'm mad at him." Did I really have to defend myself?

"It was a mistake. He thought he had a sure bet."

Always defending Dad. It was getting old. "Stop it. He always thinks it's a sure bet. But it never is. Has he ever won anything more than a free drink at O'Malley's?"

"He won a car once. When you were born. That's why he thinks you're his good luck charm."

I knew about the car since Dad liked to bring it up

every time I told him he never won anything. "That was over twenty years ago."

I heard Des open the trailer door in the background, the screeching noise unmistakable.

"Oh shit, not again."

My heart missed a beat at his words. "He's not there, is he?"

"He's probably just gone out to get some coffee. I must have missed him when I was taking a shower. I'm sure he'll be back soon."

"No, he won't. Thanks anyway. I'll talk to you later."

"Now, honey, don't jump to conclusions. This might not mean anything."

I hung up without saying goodbye, because there really wasn't anything left to say. We both knew that the second Garret Montgomery disappeared, something was seriously wrong.

And the fact that he didn't call me himself made my whole body sweat. It definitely didn't mean anything good.

I snuck out of the building and into my car, hoping nobody would notice I was gone.

18

"Ma'am, are you aware that you were going ten miles over the speed limit? I'm going to need to see your driver's license."

I knew I should have slowed down going past Venter Avenue. The cops always sat there. It was close to the coffee shop, not too far from the station. Ideal location. And lots of idiots, myself included, who tried to make the light before it turned red.

"Was I? I didn't realize. I always stick to the speed limit."

The police officer looked at me with a frown, and it was clear this wasn't the first time he'd heard that line. He went back to his cruiser to check my license and took his sweet time about it. I watched the minutes tick by, and when he didn't reappear after ten minutes, I got out of the car. Bad mistake. Very bad mistake.

"Ma'am, you need to get back in your car," he shouted and drew a gun on me. A fucking gun. As if I was going to hurt him just to get out of him writing me a lousy ticket.

I held up my hand in a placating gesture. "I really

need to be somewhere. If you could just give me my ticket and send me on my way, I'd appreciate it."

"Get back in your car."

"Who died and made you the boss," I grumbled but did as I was told. It would be hard to help Dad if I was shot thanks to Officer I-take-my-job-too-seriously.

At least my move seemed to speed things up, and he came back a few minutes later. I looked at him and didn't like what I found. He didn't have my license or a ticket.

"Are you aware that you have ten overdue parking fines and three speeding tickets, all of which you acquired within the last two months?"

"Impossible. I never speed." I was so going to hell. Or at the least my nose would grow so big I would be able to dry my laundry on it.

"I have to keep your license and you will need to pay your fines or this will go to court. Once you pay your fines, you can get your car back from the impound yard on Second Street."

Shit, that was a big chunk of money I was supposed to come up with. I grabbed my bag and climbed out of my car. At least I was only a few blocks from my apartment.

After another lecture on the importance of sticking to the speed limit and not parking in front of a fire hydrant, I was sent on my merry way. The least they could have done is offer me a ride, but apparently a break-in was more urgent, and they had to go. Fine. What did I care?

I checked my phone and found a text from Jacob.

4576 N Lincoln Ave.

I didn't know if he wanted a reply, but I felt I

somehow had to acknowledge the text, because that's how it worked when you had manners.

I typed out a quick *OK* and hit Send.

When I looked down again to make sure the message had gone through, I tripped and nearly made close acquaintance with a trash can.

Instead of sending *OK*, the message read: *I like big butts and I cannot lie*

I quickly typed another message, hoping he hadn't read this one.

I didn't mean to say that. I meant to say OK

I hit send and the *OK* had once again changed to *I like big butts and I cannot lie.* This could not be happening. Not now, but really not ever. I tried again, this time spelling the *OK* out to *okay*.

And what did you know, it worked. Someone must have messed with my autocorrect. Cursing, I sprinted down the road, praying I would make it on time.

I rushed inside my apartment, out of breath and without a plan. What did someone take to go and rescue their dad?

I was distracted from my mental inventory when a sharp little bark sounded and a ball of fur came racing into my apartment. "Hey, Churchill," I greeted Mrs. Winters's puppy.

He raced past me and up on my couch to attack one of my pillows. Cute little puppy had just turned into a demon dog. "No, stop that. I still need them." I tried to get my pillow back, and after a few tugs back and forth, managed to save most of it.

There was another bark and a loud noise, and the little demon was racing past me with something pink in his mouth. I didn't own any dog toys, and whatever he

was holding had been under my couch. Which meant …
"Noooooo. Come back here."

Of course I was too slow to stop the hellhound from escaping. He easily dodged my attempts at tackling him and raced out the door. I heaved myself up from the floor where I had landed after my missed tackle and followed, slamming my door shut on the way to prevent further theft.

We raced down the stairs, but the little beast was fast for having such short legs. He disappeared inside Mrs. Winters's apartment, and I stopped at the door and knocked. "Hello, anyone home?"

Mrs. Winters appeared, her puppy nowhere to be found. "Mrs. Winters, sorry to disturb you, but Churchill stole a toy from my apartment. Can I go and get it from him?"

She opened the door and stepped back. "Of course, dear. I didn't know you had a dog yourself. What's his name?"

My cheeks turned red, and I grimaced at her. "No. No, I don't have a dog. Just the toy."

I walked past and called for the little miscreant. "Here puppy, puppy, puppy. I'll give you lots of treats and buy you a new toy if you come here now."

The promise seemed to work when Churchill came charging out of the living room and barreled into my legs, but without the toy. Friggin' fuck, I did not have time for this. "Where's your toy, little man? Did you leave it in your bed?"

A check of the dog bed turned up a ripped-up tissue and half a bone, but no bright pink vibrator.

"Is this what you're looking for, dear?" Mrs. Winters asked.

There it was, my pink bullet, getting waved around like it was a glow stick at an Enrique Iglesias concert.

"Yes, it is. Thank you, Mrs. Winters." I took it from her, careful not to meet her eyes. "I better go. I'm running late."

I stuffed the vibrator in my front pocket, at least as much as it would allow me to. The top was hanging out slightly, but what could you do? I had to go.

I left the apartment and pulled my bike out from behind the stairway. It looked just as old and beaten up as always, but at least it still had air in the tires, something I had learned long ago not to take for granted.

19

I PEDALED LIKE MY DAD'S LIFE DEPENDED ON IT, WHICH technically it did. The hat I had pushed on my head to ward off the cold wind had a hole, something I forgot about when I grabbed it. I had to remember to put the hole to the back next time. At the moment it was letting the wind through to my forehead.

In my haste to get out of the house, I didn't zip my jacket all the way and now had to deal with a frozen belly button and nipples. Yet I didn't feel any of it, my thoughts stuck on how I was going to save Dad and add a few zeros to the $7.40 I had in my account.

Maybe I should call Des. He seemed to have a much better grasp on his money and wasn't afraid to give it to Dad, the eternal black money hole.

I made it to the address without freezing to death. I felt like I was already winning. The red brick building housed a pizza place, a pharmacy, and some kind of sex store. The address on my phone told me to go to shop 3, the restaurant.

I rested my bike against the wall, not bothering with a lock. Let's be realistic; nobody would steal my old rusty piece of junk unless they were desperate. And blind.

The door was unlocked despite the closed sign, and I walked inside. A bell announced my entry, and four heads turned in my direction. None of them familiar, all of them of the neckless variety.

One of them came over and patted me down, faltering slightly when he came across the vibrator in my pocket. *Yeah, I didn't know where I was going with that one either, buddy, so stop judging me.*

"Sit down," Brute One commanded and pointed to a seat at the table.

Goody, I'll be included in their round of Russian roulette.

"I'm supposed to meet your boss. Is he around?" I asked before my ass had even met the seat.

Silence. That's all I got. And then we sat there in—you guessed it—more silence. An awkward, "should I say something or keep fiddling with the thread that is hanging off my jacket sleeve" silence.

I lasted about seventy seconds. I knew because I watched the clock. "So who wants to play a round of Go Fish?"

More silence, but I did get one raised eyebrow. Right.

"So no Go Fish. How about Uno?"

I was once again met with crickets. Deciding that was as much awkward silence as my overactive brain could handle, I stood up. Immediately guns were drawn, and my chair fell to the ground when I backed into it.

My arms went up, and I looked to Brute One. I felt like we had a connection before. He was also the only one who had said anything to me at all. "As much fun as this has been, I should really talk to your boss and get out of your hair."

Guns went back into their holsters and pants, but nobody sat down. I eyed the door and considered making a run for it. Coming here on my own and not telling anyone what I was doing had been phenomenally stupid. I had done a lot of stupid shit in my life, but this one took first place in Willa's *award of ideas that should never have seen the light of day*.

"Sit down," Brute One said. He was the only one still with his gun out, a gun that was now pointing at the seat. I guess he won that argument, since he had a gun and all. So I sat back down, adjusted the vibrator in my pocket that was sticking into my thigh uncomfortably, and tapped my fingers on the table.

One scathing look from one of the brutes, and I dropped my hand like they'd stuck a knife in it. They might if I pissed them off enough.

Another minute went past agonizingly slow and the scenarios in my head on what had happened to Dad were getting out of hand. What if they chopped off his hand? His ear? Or tortured him. Water torture. Removed fingernails. Hung him upside down from the ceiling.

I was getting hot from all the worrying and tugged at my clothes. Wearing a jacket and hat inside made my body temperature rise to uncomfortable levels. The hat went first, but I was still burning up.

After another thirty seconds of sitting in silence, I moved my upper body forward, because heaven forbid I stand up again, unzipped my jacket, and put a hand on the inside to push it off.

Despite my good intentions, all guns were drawn again and my hands froze. "Just taking my jacket off, guys, not trying to get out a bomb. Fuck, you need to relax."

Turned out mentioning a bomb to a room full of beefed-up bad guys was the wrong thing to do. Story of my life really, so I wasn't surprised when I was tackled to the ground and the jacket was ripped off me.

"If you wanted to give me a hand, we could have done this standing up." My voice was muffled since my cheek was pressed to the floor.

After inspecting my jacket, they stood me back up. The shuffle had unearthed the vibrator, and it tumbled to the floor with a loud clank. All eyes went to the pink bullet, and I wished I *had* brought a bomb instead.

I leaned down and picked it up, not meeting anyone's eyes. Back into my jeans pocket it went, still not small enough to fit, but what can you do? I don't know why I even bothered getting embarrassed anymore. But I did, and dropping a vibrator in front of four guys was high on my list of embarrassing encounters.

"Willa," a deep and vaguely familiar voice called out. I turned and was met with a stunning specimen of the male gender. Blonde tousled hair, green eyes, and a body that was used to working out a few hours each day. He looked almost as hot as Jameson: they could have been brothers, their height and bone structure eerily similar. But I knew that Jameson only had one brother. The voice was the same as the one on the phone, so I presumed I was looking at the guy my dad owed money to.

His next words confirmed it. "Glad you could make it. I'm Jacob." He held out his arm. "Shall we?"

I definitely did not take his arm, hand, or any other appendage he was offering. What I did do was stumble and need his help anyway to prevent a face-plant. He led me to an office in the back and deposited me on a chair opposite his desk, taking a seat on the other side.

I felt like I had stepped onto the set of Dracula. The walls were black, the carpet red, and the desk a deep mahogany. It was polished to perfection.

I was thrown so far off I didn't even have a smart-ass comment at the ready. And I wondered what Dad had gotten himself involved in, because this office reeked of money.

"Your dad owes me money." He leaned forward, his focus on me, not something I particularly enjoyed since it meant he expected me to fix whatever my dad had messed up. "A lot of money, which according to him he can't pay back. And now he's disappeared."

Of course he did. "I figured as much. And now you want me to pay it back. Well, I can cut this whole thing short. I don't have the money. I won't be able to get the money. And I will definitely not cover for my dad. It's his debt; he needs to pay it off."

Jacob stared at me but didn't respond. He was starting to make me feel uncomfortable. I wiped at my face to make sure I didn't have any mascara smudges, but he continued staring.

"Everything okay?" I asked, just to get him to stop staring.

"Did you know that your mouth is blue?"

Fuck it all, I totally forgot about the blue-mouth issue while I was busy fearing for my life. No wonder the beefed-up hard-asses outside were staring. "It's food color. Should be gone in a few hours."

He seemed thrown off his big badass course, and his lips twitched but didn't allow for a full smile. His features were back under control again within seconds.

"Since he's vanished into thin air, you're all I've got. Call him."

As if I hadn't tried that already as soon as I'd heard

from Jacob, but since he asked so nicely, I pulled my phone out of my back pocket and called Dad. It went to voice mail after four rings, and I left a message. "Dad, it's Willa. You need to call me as soon as you get this."

I hung up and looked expectantly at Jacob, hoping my job here was done. "Can I go now?"

"You will stay until I talk to him."

"But I have to go to work. They'll wonder where I am. Call the cops. File a missing person's report."

He didn't look impressed. "Tell them you're sick."

"I'm never sick. And my dickweasel boss writes me up if I give him so much as a sneeze at the wrong time. This is going to lose me my job." Even though working at a diner wasn't my dream occupation, it did help to pay the bills. I wasn't too excited to have to find another minimum-wage job.

"Not my problem."

There wasn't really anything else to say, and Jacob went back to work on his computer. I sat back down with a loud sigh and dialed the Donut Hole. Lucky for me, Anita answered. "Donut Hole, how can I help you?"

"Anita, it's Willa." I sniffled and coughed dramatically, and Jacob shook his head at me. "I'm not feeling well. Can you get someone to cover for me tonight?"

"He's going to fire you if you don't show up. He's in a mood today."

"He's always in a mood. It's called being an asshole. Can you at least try and talk to him? Pretty please with free dinner on top?"

"Sure, honey. But you better start applying for a new job."

I hung up, knowing that I had just lost my job. Dad

better have a damn good explanation on why I was stuck in Dracula's lair, trying to sort out his epic fuckup.

After an hour of sitting in the antique chair, my ass hurt and my thumb was numb from playing Angry Birds. A glance at Jacob confirmed he was busy on his computer, and I moved to the couch. He looked up briefly when I relocated my butt but didn't say anything. Two hours later, I was lying on my back, my phone now drained of its battery thanks to a few too many rounds of Tetris, staring holes at the ceiling.

I had moved from scared out of my brains to bored out of my brains. And bored, in my books, equaled bad decisions. Always.

I got up and started pacing the room, picking up random objects. Samurai sword, a paper weight heavier than my handbag, and an antique-looking urn. Unable to keep quiet any longer, I said, "He's not going to call me back."

Jacob lifted his head from behind his screen, unimpressed. "He will eventually if he wants to see you again."

That sounded ominous. And scary. "Look, you need to give him time to come up with the money. How about a payment plan?"

"Do I look like I give out payment plans?" Nope, he certainly did not. What he did look was pissed off. Should have kept my mouth shut and waited this out. Maybe I could catch up on my sleep while he was busy being the bad guy.

"Nope. Definitely not. Sorry I asked. I'll just go back to the couch. Maybe have a nap. And definitely not say another word. It will be like I'm not even in the room. I can be as quiet as a church mouse, which I will be." I looked up into his way-too-symmetrical features and realized how he was the boss. All that pretty exterior? Not so pretty when he pointed his gun at you and looked like he was one word away from going into a murderous rage. His face was set in stone, beautiful but angry stone. So I shut up and sat down.

Something else occurred to me at that moment. How was Dad going to call me back if my phone was dead? What if he had already tried? I lifted my hand like a good kid in school and waited for Jacob to notice me. He did eventually, my arm getting lower and lower with every minute that passed. I really had to get back to the gym.

"What now?" He sounded annoyed. But annoyed I could work with. Annoyed was an emotion I had all too much experience with.

"My phone is dead."

"For fuck's sake, are you trying to make me shoot you?"

"No, absolutely not. But you don't happen to have a charger anywhere do you?"

"Bill," he yelled out to the door.

Brute One came in, looking as brutely as always. "Boss."

"Get her a charger for her phone."

He held out his hand, and I stared at it. Did he want me to get up?

"Phone," he growled, making me jump and hand my phone over like it didn't have my whole life on it. He left the room but didn't close the door.

There was conversation outside, but I was unable to make out what they said. Brute One came back with a charger and my phone and plugged them both into the wall next to Jacob's desk.

He left without another word, this time closing the

door, and the room was again cased in silence. After a few minutes, I went over to the desk and turned my phone back on. As soon as it came alive, I was assaulted with text messages and voice mails.

A scroll through showed none were from my dad, but nearly all from Jameson and Maisie. I scrolled though the texts first. Maisie was back from London and wanted to catch up. I texted her back first, making plans for tomorrow.

Jameson's texts on the other hand weren't as easy to deal with.

JAMESON: *Where did you go?*

Jameson: *Don't be mad at Landon. He said he's sorry he made your mouth blue. Call me.*

Jameson: *I'm getting worried.*

Jameson: *Now I'm officially worried.*

Jameson: *Where are you?*

Jameson: *Answer your phone.*

Jameson: *You can't possibly be angry at me for something Landon did. Talk to me.*

THAT WAS THE LAST MESSAGE, sent only two minutes ago. I typed out a response to prevent Jameson from coming after me.

ME: *I'm ok, don't worry. I'll call you later.*

I HIT Send and looked at Jacob. "No calls from my dad."

He studied my features and snatched my phone from my hand. It was still unlocked, and Jameson's texts were open. He scrolled through the messages, ignoring my attempts at getting the phone back.

"Sit down," he said, his voice sharp and commanding. My butt automatically heeded his command, and I found myself seated on the uncomfortable antique furniture again.

"Were you sending him an encrypted message?"

"What? No. Of course not. I just told him that I was okay. Otherwise he would have started looking for me."

"You told him you like big butts. The same thing you messaged me. What does it stand for?"

Oh. The. Shame. Someone was going to die. Slowly, very slowly.

"Someone messed with my phone's autocorrect. It's not a secret message, and it doesn't mean anything other than I might go to jail in the near future after I kill the person who did this."

He studied my face and seemed to believe me when he nodded and gave me my phone back. "He replied."

I saw Jameson's response as soon as I had my phone safely back in my hands.

Jameson: *Are you drunk? Let me pick you up.*

Me: *Not drunk, just another present from Landon. No need to pick me up. I'm fine where I am.*

Jameson: *And where is that exactly?*

Me: *I gotta go. Call you later.*

My phone rang, scaring the shit out of me, and I dropped it on the floor. Jameson's name flashed on the screen. Jacob bent down to pick it up and handed it to me. "Answer it. Otherwise he'll just keep calling."

I hesitated but knew he was right. Jameson wasn't

one to give up easily. And he knew something was wrong. I hit the Answer button.

"Hey."

"What's going on? Why are you trying to avoid me?" Jameson sounded hurt. It made my little sarcastic heart wail in agony.

"I'm not trying to avoid you. I'm just busy. At work."

"You're not at work. I went to the Donut Hole. Your boss said he fired you."

"I got a new job. At a restaurant."

"What restaurant?"

"A place near Hester Ave."

"What's it called?"

"You wouldn't know it. I really need to get back. Don't want to get fired on my first day. I'll talk to you tomorrow."

"Don't—"

I cut him off by hanging up. I left the phone on the desk and flopped onto the couch.

"Jameson knows you're lying to him," Jacob said, never lifting his gaze from his computer screen.

"And how would you know?"

"He's smart, and he obviously cares about you. No way did he buy your little story."

Did everyone in this godforsaken town know each other?

"He doesn't know where I am. And he is not going to call me back. Jameson is one of the most prideful men I have ever met. I'd be surprised if he still has my number by tomorrow."

Jacob lifted the corner of his mouth in a half smile. "We'll see."

Another hour went past agonizingly slow. My phone was almost fully charged, but it hadn't made a beep since Jameson called. There had been no further contact on his part, but who could blame him.

I heard a crash outside and sat up. Jacob was already at the door, gun drawn. He opened it slowly and cursed. "Fucking should have known." He turned to me. "Stay here. I mean it. Do not move."

I had no intention of going out there. It sounded like someone was chopping wood out there. Or body parts. Nope, no way was I going out there.

I paced the room, jumping at every crash and yell. The commotion didn't last long, and all went silent again. Too silent. I stared at the door, going cross-eyed.

Moments later the door opened, revealing Jacob, followed by another person. "Look for yourself. She's fine. Now can you calm the fuck down and stop destroying my furniture?" Jacob said, sounding annoyed at the inconvenience. Personally, I would be freaking out if someone came into my restaurant and trashed the place.

My mouth dropped open, and my eyes went wide when I saw he was talking to Jameson. Brain shutdown was all I could think before he crossed the room in three long strides—damn those muscly legs—and stopped in front of me.

"Did he touch you? Are you hurt? If he laid a finger on you, he's a dead man walking."

I put my hand to his cheek, which stopped his rant abruptly, and the contact made me feel a million times better. "What are you doing here?"

His hands roamed my body as if he had to assure himself that I was still in one piece. He brushed over the vibrator, and I shrugged in response to his raised eyebrow.

"As heartwarming as this reunion is, I have a business to run. Currently I'm ten grand in the negative thanks to her dad. Now that you saw she's in one piece I would appreciate it if you didn't continue to take my restaurant apart. And she's staying until I can get my hands on Garret."

"I'll pay you the money. You know I'm good for it."

I went ramrod straight and glared at Jameson. He could not pay off Dad's debt. Absolutely not. "No, you won't. I'll stay here until Dad calls me back, which he will. Eventually."

I made a move to sit down, but Jameson stopped me by putting his arm around me and pulling me into his side. "He won't show his face because he doesn't have the money. I know he doesn't. You know he doesn't." He pointed at Jacob. "He knows he doesn't."

I tried to extract myself from his embrace, but he held firm. "Once he listens to his messages, he'll call me back and sort it all out. You'll see. It will be fine."

Both men ignored my protests and talked to each other like I wasn't there. "Transfer the money. If I don't have it by tomorrow, I'll come back for her," Jacob said.

Jameson nodded at him. "Thanks, man, appreciate it."

Jacob went back to his desk, and Jameson led me out the door after he picked up my phone and bag. One of Jacob's guys was holding an ice pack to his face, and one of the tables was smashed. The room looked otherwise untouched. We were outside before I could do more than gape.

"What are you doing?" I asked, irritated at being manhandled.

"Getting you the hell out of there. What were you thinking coming here by yourself? Have you lost your mind?"

I stepped out of his tight hold and took my bag and phone from him. "No, I haven't. And I didn't need your help. I had it all under control."

Jameson followed my every movement, not willing to let me escape. "Where is your car?"

"None of your business."

"I fixed it, so if it broke down again, it is very much my business since that would mean I did a shit job."

"It didn't break down." I righted my bike and stashed my phone in my back pocket. "It got impounded."

"Say what?"

I was not going to repeat myself, especially not when he looked like he was ready to burst out laughing. "It's not funny."

"Why would the cops impound your car?"

"Missed a few ticket payments. Now can I go?" I tried to push my bike around him, but he was still having none of it.

"No, you can't go. I want to know why you're avoiding me."

"You just paid my dad's debt."

"And?"

"It was my responsibility, not yours. And how do you propose I'm going to pay you back?"

"You are still working for me. I'll dock your pay and we're good."

He was impossible. "That would take me ages."

"That's fine with me." He put his big arms around me, and I didn't put up much of a fight when he pulled me to him. I was tired. Tired of keeping my shit together, tired of taking care of Dad.

I was still holding on to my bike with one hand, but

the other went around his neck. As soon as I made contact, my world looked a lot brighter.

"How did you not get shot in there anyway? And how did you know where I was?"

"Jacob's my cousin. His mom would have killed him if he had shot me. And there is only one restaurant near Hester Ave."

I pulled back, stunned. "He's your cousin? But he's a criminal."

Jameson raised a brow at me. "You do know how your dad got his debt to me, right?"

Illegal car racing, as if I could forget. And if rumors were true, Mason was the mastermind behind the whole operation. I wondered how much Jameson was involved.

Defeated and out of ideas on how to get Dad back, I got on my bike. "I have to find Dad. I'll call you later. I'm sorry."

I started pedaling, trying hard to ignore Jameson's protests, but looked back at him anyway. In doing so I was distracted and ran into something, falling off my bike.

Jameson plucked me off the ground. "You are a walking, talking disaster. How the hell did you make it through life in one piece?" He checked me for injuries, something he seemed to be doing an awful lot lately. "Did you hurt yourself?"

I flexed my arms and wiggled my legs, but other than a few bruises, I would be just fine. However, the person that I had run into didn't seem so great. They were still on the ground, not sounding too flush. Groaning was never a good sign.

I bent down to help them up and noticed that of all the people that could have stood in my way, I had to hit a police officer. "Sir, I'm so, so sorry. Let me help you up."

I reached out, but he swatted my hand away. "Stay away from me. Don't you know you're not allowed to ride your bike on a sidewalk?"

"I didn't realize you were there."

I tried helping him up again, but he was having none of it. "Ma'am, step back or I'll arrest you."

Talk about an overreaction. "Arrest me? But it was an accident. And I'm trying to help you."

Another voice joined us, this one even less friendly. "Ma'am, step away from the police officer. Put your hands over your head and get on your knees."

Instead of doing what I was told, I stupidly asked, "Sorry, what?"

"Get down on your knees with your hands over your head."

"That's ridiculous. It was an accident. I didn't mean to run into anyone."

"Ma'am, I won't ask you again."

Jameson stepped forward, but found the gun formerly pointed at me now directed at him. "Sir, I have to ask you to step away and not interfere in a police operation."

"Officer, this is a misunderstanding. There is no need for handcuffs. I'm sure a ticket will be enough in this case." Jameson looked irritated.

I was still not kneeling, but avidly staring at the police officer. I knew him. Had gone to school with him. "Ray, there really is no need for guns."

"It's Officer Ray to you."

I grumbled but got down on my knees to speed things up. Knowing him and his love of superiority, he would make me pay for my insubordination.

"You're under arrest. You have the right to remain silent. Anything you say.... Gun! Gun!" He patted me down but froze when he got to the fucking vibrator. I should have thrown it in the trash. Hindsight and all that.

And this is how I found myself facedown on the asphalt because Officer Dick thought I had a gun in my pocket.

20

I ENDED UP GETTING ARRESTED.

"Is this really necessary?" I asked for the third time, wiggling my cuffed hands behind my back. "It's not like you don't know where I live. Do you really think I'd make a run for it?"

"It's procedure."

Procedure, my ass. This was payback for the time in third grade when I wouldn't let him play catch with us. "So why did I watch you lead Milton into your car without cuffing him after he started a fight at the Donut Hole?"

"The circumstances were different. Now shut up and get out of the car." Ray was standing next to the open door, one hand on my arm the other on the door, ready to help me up and inside the police station.

"Fine. But I'm not spending the night in a jail cell. If Milton didn't have to, then I won't either."

"You are just as big of a pain as always," he grumbled.

I grinned my most obnoxious grin at him, the one with a lot of teeth and not much face. Ray's eyes went wide, and he stared at me. "What happened to your mouth? It's blue."

Said mouth snapped closed, and I shut up. Guess it took more than a few hours to get rid of the blue. He led me to the big, open-plan office and sat me down on a chair. "Someone will be with you shortly."

"I want to talk to my lawyer."

"You don't have a lawyer."

"How would you know?"

He shot me a look, and I shot one back at him. No need to get personal.

He rolled his eyes and walked away. At least he had removed my cuffs.

Getting arrested by the Humptulips Police Department meant that by tomorrow the whole town would know about it. Thanks to Dad's frequent arrests, everyone and their dog knew our family. The gossips would go crazy over my arrest since the daughter finally joined her dad in the family tradition.

Twenty-one years without an arrest. I thought I hit a low point when I got a perm that took over a year to grow out. Guess I didn't know shit back then. I sank into the chair and waited for whoever was stuck with my paperwork. But instead of an officer, Jameson showed up.

"Come on, let's go."

He held out his hand, but all I was capable of doing was stare at it. If he was breaking me out, he had to pry me out of this chair kicking and screaming. Prison breaks weren't my style, and I was staying.

"They know where I live," I said.

Jameson wrinkled his forehead in confusion. "What does it matter?"

"They'll find me."

"Why would they try and find you?"

"Because you're breaking me out?"

That's when he started laughing, his voice booming, the sound entirely too pleasant for my dire situation. Didn't he understand that I was about to be put into a jail cell?

"I'm not breaking you out. You're free to go. Weren't you wondering why you're not cuffed anymore?"

I was wondering about that but just thought that Ray might have found his tiny black heart. Apparently he didn't have a heart at all, since he didn't tell me that I was free to go.

"That bastard. He told me to wait here."

Jameson took my hand and pulled me out of the chair. "Come on, let's get you home."

Jameson's truck was parked in the police department's parking lot, and like the gentleman he was, he helped me into my seat, brushing my butt a few times in the process.

I pouted all the way back to my apartment. It was childish and unnecessary. I knew that. But I also felt like, if there was ever a good time to pout, it was now. I screwed up not only going to Jacob by myself without telling anyone but by being an ungrateful brat to Jameson. He saved my bacon, and I told him off.

Then he got me out of an arrest. Wait, how did he get me out, exactly?

We pulled up to my apartment, and Jameson parked his massive truck expertly in one of the tiny parking spaces. Before he had a chance to open his door, I stopped him with a hand on his arm. "How did you make them drop the charges? I pissed them off good this time."

He leaned in closer and pressed a kiss to my lips.

Gentle, soft, perfect. I think I sighed but couldn't be too sure. "I called in a favor." He got out and rounded the truck to open my door. "Let's get you inside."

He helped me out of the truck, and I secretly enjoyed his big hands on my body. I never considered myself tiny, but I was compared to Jameson. He took my hand as soon as my feet hit the ground and walked me inside. Mrs. Winters's door opened as we walked past, and she emerged decked out in her boots and thick fur coat. She never left the house without it, not even on a ninety-degree day. Churchill was bouncing along beside her, biting his lead.

"Hello, dear. How was your day? I hope we didn't make you too late for your appointment," she said.

"Good evening, Mrs. Winters. I made it just in time."

"You have to let me know where you got the dog toy from. I have to get one for Winston Churchill. He loved it."

"I don't remember where I bought it," I mumbled, my face turning red.

"That's okay, my dear." She turned towards her dog. "Come on, let's go outside and practice going to the toilet somewhere that isn't my apartment."

As soon as the door closed behind them, Jameson burst out laughing. I shook my head at him and grabbed his arm, dragging him along with me. "Let's get inside. I can't deal with anything else today."

"It wasn't all that bad. There were at least a few memorable moments." He had moved closer, and we were walking up the stairs with my back pressed to his front. His hands trailed my stomach, and I could feel a growing bulge digging into my back. He pulled me closer, and my steps faltered.

"They couldn't have been that memorable since I seem to have forgotten all about them."

We reached my apartment door, Jameson stopped me, turned me around, and pinned me to the door. "Then I guess I'll just have to remind you."

He leaned down and pressed his mouth to mine. I opened immediately, and the kiss turned from a reminder into a scorcher. Of all the things Jameson was good at, kissing topped that list. And he was damn good at a lot of things.

I fumbled with the door, and after failing to open it while kissing Jameson, I broke away and unlocked my door. As soon as it gave way, Jameson lifted me up and my legs wound around him.

A throat clearing stopped Jameson's hands that were travelling up my shirt and made us pull apart. I looked inside my apartment and at my Dad.

"What the hell are you doing here?" I snapped at him, furious. "I was looking everywhere for you. Do you know how much shit you got me in?"

He stood up from where he was sitting on my old couch and approached but stopped when I held up my hand. "You owe Jameson ten thousand dollars."

Dad looked embarrassed. "I'll pay him back. I just don't have the money right now."

I couldn't keep the bitterness out of my voice when I responded. "Of course you don't. Because if you did, I wouldn't have had to spend the last five hours sitting on Jacob's couch, hoping nobody put a bullet through my head."

"I'm sorry, honey, but you know how it is."

"Yes, I know all too well. And I know something else. I'm done. You can't keep dragging me into your mess. Until you get your shit together, I'm done." I stepped out of the hallway and pointed to the front door. "Get out."

"Willa—"

"Now. I don't want you in my apartment. Don't call me, and stop involving me in your shit."

He heard the finality in my voice and walked out, leaving a muttered, "I'm sorry, honey," in his wake.

I watched Dad leave and closed the door as soon as he was in the hallway. Jameson had stepped inside and was watching me but stayed quiet. Never before had I cut Dad out of my life, but I couldn't do it anymore. The first tear trickled down my cheek, and I wiped it away angrily. Why was I feeling so sad if he deserved everything I said to him?

I was confused and angry at myself for not doing something sooner. My life was a mess. And I had let it get to this point. Suddenly Jameson was there, putting his big arms around me and pulling me into his hard chest.

I buried my head in his neck and let out a deep sigh. I didn't know how I would be able to let go of him once he was ready to move on.

"Let me take care of you tonight," he said, resting his cheek on my head.

I sniffled into his chest. "Will it involve pizza?"

He hugged me closer. "Definitely. And if you're lucky, I'll throw in some beer."

He made good on his promise and ordered three large pizzas. Jameson didn't mess around. He said he would take care of me, and he did. He even bought beer. Now some might think that was selfish of him, but they wouldn't know how much I loved it. And for some reason, Jameson knew that.

He seemed to know a lot about me. My favorite

movie—Lethal Weapon—my favorite dessert—any cupcake I could get my hands on. He even knew my favorite pizza toppings—pretty much anything they can fit on one large pizza.

We were camped out on my couch, watching Mel Gibson get blown up. It was the perfect night. I was full, slightly tipsy, and leaning against Jameson. He pulled me close as soon as we sat down and started playing with my hair, trailing his finger down my arm. I was in a Jameson-induced fog and had no intention of emerging.

After finishing off the pizza, I buried myself into his side and rested my beer on his lap. His hand was now buried underneath my shirt. I didn't recall the moment he had gotten in there but couldn't say I objected.

"Will you stay?" I asked before I lost my nerve. I wouldn't have asked at all if it hadn't been for the fog I was under.

"Do you want me to stay?"

I moved my head to look at him. "Yes."

He leaned down and kissed me in response. The kiss was soft and over too soon, leaving me wanting more.

"Then I will," he said simply.

I sat up and put my beer on the table. Jameson watched my every move, probably questioning my sudden activity after my bout of lethargy. I turned back to him and lifted a leg over his lap so I was facing him. My hands found their way into his T-shirt, pulling it over his head.

"Thank you for your help today." I should have said this earlier, but my pride wouldn't let me. But his unwavering support was overwhelming. Sure, I had my friends who I knew would drop everything and come to my rescue if I had asked. But somehow it felt different with Jameson. He seemed ready for whatever curveball I threw at him. He seemed to wait for it and was ready to catch it when I needed him to.

"I'll pay you back the money. This time I'll be actually working it off. I'm sorry I got mad at you."

A smile hovered on his lips. "How sorry?"

I kissed him, deep and long, wanting him to know how much he meant to me. I pushed closer, the feel of his body on mine almost too much. He was perfection in a muscly, huge package. He tugged my shirt up, and I broke the kiss to pull it off. "Very sorry."

Once my shirt was gone, I leaned back in, but Jameson stopped me, brushing his lips to mine. "I want you to know that this is so much more to me than just sex. You turned my world upside down, and I never want it the right way up again." I felt his lips moving with every word, the slight brush sending tingles from my lips all the way to my toes.

Damn, I must be a good kisser if that was his reaction. His words invaded my heart and settled deep, taking root. "Good thing I kind of like you then," I responded.

The smile that broke out on his face was a thing of beauty, an image I wanted to engrave on my brain and never forget. He didn't let me stare at him for long but instead stood up, holding me in his arms. "Bedroom?"

I pointed to one of the two doors in my small apartment. One bedroom, one bathroom, big enough to not feel like I was living in a sardine can.

He pushed the door open and dropped me on the bed, following close behind, bracing his fall with his hands on either side of my pliable body. I snort-giggled at him, the sound echoing through the room, and I slapped a hand over my face to stop the noise from escaping.

He peeled my hand away from my face, holding it. "Don't hide who you are from me."

I knew he didn't just mean the failed giggle slash snort, and I fell a little more for him. I hoped there was a soft landing at the bottom, because this girl was going down fast.

Jameson made quick work of my pants, leaving me only in my underwear. I'd love to be able to say it was black lace, but in reality I had on a bright pink bra with white hearts and purple boy shorts with a handprint on the back. He grinned when he saw my choice of underwear and trailed kisses from my neck down, paying close attention to the area not covered by my bra.

I shivered every time his mouth made contact with my skin. Goose bumps were taking permanent residence over my whole body, and I shivered. "You cold?" he asked, stopping his ministrations and lifting his head.

"Not at all," I replied, breathless.

Satisfied with my response, he continued his task, raining kisses on my chest, paying special attention to my nipples, making me squirm on the bed. He stopped my movements by placing his big hands on each side of my torso, brushing his thumbs along the side of my breasts.

"You are beautiful," he said, and brushed his lips against the corner of my mouth. "And mine. Don't ever forget that." Another brush of his lips, this time behind my ear. "I take care of what's mine."

And boy, did he ever. I guess the whole ban on licking him was now moot and dead. There would definitely be licking in his future.

21

THE BLARING OF MY ALARM RIPPED ME OUT OF THE WARM cocoon Jameson's body created. My hand emerged from under the sheets, blindly slapping at my phone.

"Too early." Jameson's voice was muffled since he insisted on burying his head in my boobs. I tried to wiggle out from underneath him, but his arms tightened, and he complained, "Not yet."

I brushed my hand through his thick hair, enjoying the soft feel of it. "I have to go to work. You have to find another pillow."

"There really is no better pillow than your boobs." He nuzzled his face into the valley between my breasts, and I arched into him like a cat.

"I'm running late."

"So what's a few more minutes?"

His mouth travelled down my stomach, and I squirmed underneath him. "A few minutes?"

He lifted his head to look at me. "I'll take what I can get. Even a minute with you is more than I ever hoped for."

Heart. Melted. He sure was laying it on thick this

morning. "You don't have to butter me up to get laid. I'm already giving you free access."

"Free access? I like the sound of that." He lowered his head again, and I liked the way this morning was going.

The ringing of my alarm ripped me out of my happy thoughts and back into reality. I couldn't let Rayna down, and I would already be late.

"I'm sorry, Jameson." I sat up, and he did the same. I moved my feet to the side, but he stopped my movements by taking my hand. "Just promise not to disappear on me again."

I looked back over my shoulder at him and raised a brow. "I won't. Promise."

He kissed my shoulder. "You know I'll just come after you. Now that I know how good things can be, I won't just let go."

I shook my head and gave his hand a squeeze before pulling away and getting up. The task of sifting through my clothes for something that didn't smell like grease or batter took longer than anticipated. I missed laundry day again.

"If you get hungry, there might be some Cocoa Puffs in the cupboard, but I'm out of coffee. And milk," I said, walking to the bathroom.

I sped through my shower and pulled on the clothes I'd taken from the stack in my room. Jeans and T-shirt would have to do for now. My wet hair was piled on top of my head in a messy bun, and I forwent the makeup. Again.

Jameson was fast asleep when I got back to my room. The sheet was draped around his middle, and I reached out and pulled it down further. Just one little peek and I'd go. Yup, definitely worth it. I kissed his delectable ass, and his eyes opened.

"How are you going to get to work?" he asked in a raspy voice, heavy with sleep.

"Bus." Since I didn't have my car or bike anymore, it was my only option.

His eyes opened all the way, and he jumped out of bed. All I could do was stare and maybe drool a little. I mean, it was Jameson naked. One should never so much as miss a second by blinking when faced with such a glorious sight.

"I'll drive you. Just give me a minute." He could have more than a minute. What? Wait, I had to go. No more extra minutes.

He was dressed and standing in front of me before I had a chance to finish my thought or close my mouth. He pushed my jaw up and tilted my head in the process. "Eyes up here." He kissed me and took my hand. "Let's go. Might as well get a run in before work since you got me up in the middle of the night."

We left my apartment, and fifteen minutes later, he pulled up in front of Sweet Dreams. Jameson got out and opened my door before I had a chance to even lift a finger. He kissed me softly, his lips lingering. "Message me when you're done, and I'll come pick you up."

I nodded and stole one more kiss. "Thanks for the lift."

I shuffled into the store, my sights set on the coffee machine. "Sorry I'm late," I called out to Rayna, who was bent over a ginormous house-shaped cake.

"As if I haven't heard that one before," she muttered.

I hugged her side, careful not to jostle her too much

and screw up the cake. "Is that for the Fosters' house-warming?"

"It sure is. A cake that looks exactly like their house." She snorted under her breath. "They even insisted on the rosebushes."

I grabbed a cup and poured coffee, added a dash of milk, and leaned over her shoulder. The rose bushes looked amazing. She even added little thorns. "You did all that? Without calling me?"

"I have to grow up sometime. I know you won't be here forever. Who wants to work at their aunt's tiny little bakery for the rest of their lives?"

"Rayna." I waited for her to turn around and look at me. "I love working here, and I can never repay you for what you've done for me. If it wasn't for you, I'd probably be living underneath Fitzroy Bridge with Bernie. I'd happily spend the rest of my life working for you if you finally give me that pay raise that you promised."

She scoffed at me. "You'd never be homeless. And Bernie is a sweetheart. He'd let you share his sleeping bag I'm sure." Her eyes were glassy, and she pulled me into an air-stealing hug. "I love you. You're the only family I have left. I might be a bit biased, but you are one of the smartest people I know. And you have the biggest heart. Don't ever change."

I felt like a fraud and crumbled like a leaf at her words. "I'm not really. I kicked Dad out of my apartment yesterday. Told him I don't want anything to do with him." And I still felt like a horrible, horrible person about it.

Rayna pulled back, eyes big. "And now you just confirmed why I think you're awesome. I've been waiting for this day since you picked him up from the Humptulips police station for the first time."

"You really think I did the right thing?" I knew Rayna wasn't Dad's biggest fan, but I never realized how far her contempt went.

"He is forty-eight years old and more than capable of standing on his own two feet. Don't you dare feel bad about telling him to take care of his own shit."

I nodded and pushed the uneasy feeling aside. He would be fine. "I'll try. Now tell me what cakes are on the agenda today so I can make up for being late."

By the time Jameson picked me up, I was one cup of coffee away from a heart attack and covered in bits of cake and icing. "Will, lover boy is here," Rayna called through the shop as Jameson came inside. I was still cleaning up the kitchen from an earlier caramel sauce experiment gone wrong.

I dumped the ruined pot into the trash and finished wiping down the counter. After I washed the worst of the chocolate off my hands, I hung my apron on its hook next to the door. I emerged from the kitchen to find Rayna and Jameson engaged in a hushed conversation.

I feared for the worst. Rayna was a master meddler and closet romantic. She might have given up on her own love life, but that didn't mean she didn't take every opportunity to find me my happily ever after.

Jameson looked up when I approached, and the gleam in his eyes told me he didn't mind the mess I was at all. He covered the few steps we were still apart with his long strides and pulled me to him, ignoring the stains I would leave on his shirt.

Rayna winked at me when we walked past, and I made a cutting motion across my throat. She knew better than to play fairy and sprinkle her gold dust around.

"Have fun, kids. And remember: safe sex is good sex."

We made it outside to the tune of her laughter.

We settled inside the truck, and Jameson pulled away from the curb. "You're going the wrong way," I said when I noticed that we passed the gas station, which was definitely nowhere near my neighborhood.

"I have to get back to the garage, and I'm taking you with me now because I can't pick you up later. You can take a nap and clean up in my apartment."

I had a few hours left before I was due to start, thanks to the reduced hours we had negotiated. A nap sounded like heaven. A shower even better, but I didn't bring a change of clothes with me.

"I can get to the garage myself. I know how to take the bus. Learned it a while ago."

"Smart-ass. I know you can get there yourself, but I don't want you to have to take the bus when I can just take you with me now."

"I don't have a change of clothes, and I definitely need to get changed." A gaze down my shirt confirmed that it was a mess of flour, icing, and unidentifiable brown goo.

"No problem, I'll wash your clothes while you're in the shower."

Of course he would. Because he was perfect. And nice. I was waiting for the bubble to burst.

"Fine. Take me with you then."

"That's the plan."

He took my hand and placed it on his thigh as if he'd done the very same thing a million times before. My heart was full of Jameson, and he buried himself deeper with every little gesture.

We arrived, and Jameson went to the shop, and I

went to his apartment. The shower was heaven and the nap just what I needed. I loved his bed. The mattress was a fluffy cloud, the sheets felt silky against my skin, and the bed smelled like Jameson. Heaven.

I borrowed one of Jameson's T-shirts, the long material hanging down to my knees. I could honestly say that so far my day was going well. No arrests, no debts to pay off that weren't my own, and I had just woken up in a fluffy cloud, surrounded by all that was Jameson without him actually being there.

I was busy rummaging through his fridge for something to eat when the front door opened. "Where has all your food gone?" I said.

"Jameson has an aversion to grocery stores."

I shot up at the female voice. That was definitely not Jameson. Nope, the woman in front of me did look a lot like him though. Except for her clothes. And perfectly coiffed hair. Not a strand out of place. Where Jameson's wardrobe seemed to exclusively consist of jeans and T-shirts, she looked like she just came from a meeting with the queen.

I was to meet his mother, dressed in a shirt that wasn't mine, rummaging through a fridge that definitely didn't belong to me. And the day had been going so well.

The only thing I could come up with at that moment was to hold out my hand. "Mrs. Drake. So nice to meet you. I'm Willa."

She didn't take my hand. Instead she stepped forward and embraced me in a hug. I didn't move my arms at first, letting them dangle like useless logs at my side. Alternate universe. It had to be. Or I was still sleeping.

She released me and thankfully stepped back again. Personal space, people.

"I've heard so much about you," she said.

"You have?" My voice sounded suspicious because if she'd heard about me, it would have been in connection with Dad.

"The boys talk about you all the time. I'm so glad to finally meet you. Are you coming for dinner on Sunday?"

I studied her face, looking for signs that she didn't actually mean what she said. But she looked sincere, and I probably looked confused.

I didn't know how Jameson felt about me meeting his family. He didn't do girlfriends, and meeting everyone screamed girlfriend to the world. "Thank you for the invitation, but I already have plans on Sunday."

She raised a delicate hand to stop me from talking. "Nonsense. You're coming Sunday and that's that." She lifted up a hand, holding a container. "I made cake. Help yourself." She put the container on the counter and waved to me. "I'll see you Sunday."

And she was gone, leaving me to wonder how to get out of what promised to be an awkward dinner. I gave up my quest for food and went in search of my clothes instead. They were already in the dryer, ready to be put back on. Jameson must have come in while I was sleeping.

When I finally made it back into the office, I was starving. I popped my head into the garage to see if anyone else wanted anything and was greeted with loud cursing.

"Fucking phone. Make it stop." I heard a frustrated groan followed by a loud bang. "Mason, you're the tech genius. Turn it off."

I walked inside since I was pretty sure I knew why Landon was cursing up a storm. Payback was a bitch.

Mason was holding Landon's phone, snickering at the screen. "Dude, why would you sign up for Celine Dion updates?"

"I fucking didn't," Landon bellowed. "They just started popping up on my phone, and I don't know how to unsubscribe. They sing every time I open them. Do something."

"Who is hotmama666? She's offering a blowjob that will blow your mind." Mason started roaring with laughter. Landon lunged for him, trying to get his phone back, but Mason turned away and made a run for it.

"And how about somelikeitdirty who says she's been naughty and wants you to spank her?" he said from the other end of the garage. All the guys were now listening, barely containing their laughter. This was going better than even I could have anticipated. Guess the dating profile I created did its job.

Landon's face was red, and his eye twitched uncontrollably. I had definitely gotten payback and then some. I snorted when Mason continued reading the messages. My job here was done. I shouldn't have made a noise because it drew Landon's attention. Once his eyes snapped to me, they stuck like glue.

He mouthed to me, "You're going down."

I mouthed back, "Bring it on" and escaped to the safety of my office.

I hadn't been sitting on my chair for more than five minutes when Jameson came in. "It was you, wasn't it." It wasn't really a question. We both knew it was me. He plucked me out of my chair and sat down, placing me on his lap, drawing me close.

"What am I going to do with you?" He nuzzled my

ear. "Landon smashed his phone after the last message. Something about a dominatrix."

I laughed and snuggled closer. "I may have created an online dating profile for him."

"Remind me to never get on your bad side." He kissed my cheek, making me shiver.

"Just don't dye my mouth a disgusting color, and you're good."

"I think I can manage that."

I tilted my head back and wound my arms around his neck to look at him. I had to tell him that I talked to his mom and that I didn't invite myself for dinner. I wasn't that crazy. Yet. "So, your mom dropped by the apartment earlier. And she kind of invited me over for dinner on Sunday."

He touched his lips to mine, once, twice, and his tongue sneaked out, and I welcomed him without question. His hand cupped my ass, pulling me closer, and I felt his hard erection. I loved that I could do that to him. He ended the kiss when we started pulling on each other's clothes.

"I know. She came to the garage. Dinner is at six. I'll pick you up at five."

And just like that I was going to dinner with his mom. It was going to be fine. As long as I did my washing this week so I had something to wear. And acted like a normal human being. Sounded easy enough. I could keep it together for a few hours.

22

I COULD DEFINITELY NOT KEEP IT TOGETHER FOR A FEW hours. As soon as we pulled up to the farmhouse, my breathing started accelerating. I had donned my one and only black dress, opting for a conservative look to make a good second impression. Especially since I wasn't exactly dressed the first time I met his mom.

Even Jameson was wearing a collared shirt, the only concession he was willing to make, matching it with dark-washed jeans and his usual boots. He looked so good that when he picked me up, it made me scramble across the bench in his truck and onto his lap to proceed to make out with him like a horny teenager.

Not that he complained, quite the opposite really, but now we were late, and I was experiencing the shivers of the uninitiated. The Drakes were a tight-knit family. Jameson's dad died when he was little, a well-known fact around town. They were brought up by their mom, who did the best she could raising two testosterone-filled teenagers.

Mrs. Drake opened the door before Jameson had a

chance to knock and pulled him into a tight hug. After patting his cheek, she turned to me.

"Willa. So glad you could make it," she greeted me as warmly as her son.

Jameson and Mason might be closed off to outsiders, but once you breached their walls, they were loving and kind. His mom was the bomb. I was still nervous, but at least the cold sweats had stopped, and I was walking forward instead of backward.

"Come in. Mason just got here." She led the way; Jameson put his hand on my back, guiding me behind his mother.

The house was cozy, the walls filled with photos of Jameson and Mason as kids.

We entered the living room, and Mason got up from his position on a comfortable looking couch. He slapped Jameson on the back in greeting and picked me up and twirled me around. "Willa. Let the initiation into the Drake clan begin. I hope you like snake venom."

"Mason, don't scare her away," Mrs. Drake said. "Put her down."

Mason did as instructed and gently placed me back on my feet. "Don't worry, there is no snake venom. Just a lot of whiskey," he whispered in my ear before releasing me.

The conversation was easy, and the tension seeped out of my body until Mrs. Drake started talking about their Christmas Party. "You will love it Willa. Everyone gets together, and there is lots and lots of food. Even eggnog, if that's what you're into."

"She'll be there," Jameson answered for me, and I nearly choked on my own spit. I hope he realized that it was FIVE MONTHS AWAY.

I gave him my version of a puzzled look, both brows

raised, because come on people, it was simply too hard to do the whole one-eyebrow thing. He squeezed his arm around me in response and pulled me closer, kissing my head. Another thing I loved about him. If he wanted to touch me, he did it without reservation and without care of where we were.

I sank into his side, letting the conversation flow around me and enjoying just being close to him. Dinner was amazing; Jameson cooked the steak outside on the grill while I helped his mom prepare the salad and potatoes. Dessert was a pineapple upside-down cake that melted in your mouth. There was no awkwardness to be found, the family clearly comfortable with each other. They included me into their conversations, and I found myself having fun.

They were nice. Really nice. And they genuinely cared. I loved every minute of being there, being part of a family who had dinner together, who shared what they did during the week, who made sure everyone was okay.

I never realized all that I had missed out on, but one night with the Drakes showed me what life could have been like.

Jameson noticed I had gone quiet, and he put his hand on my leg under the table and leaned closer. "Are you okay?" He studied my face, and what he saw didn't seem to please him. "What's wrong?"

"I'm good, just tired."

He didn't hesitate and said, "Then we'll go home."

He turned to his mom and got up. "It's getting late, so we'd better head off. Thanks for dinner." He hugged her tight. "See you next week. Mason, don't forget to get the Charger done tomorrow. Steve wants to pick it up on Tuesday."

Mason grumbled under his breath, sounding something like an agreement, and after Mrs. Drake pulled me to her and whispered in my ear how happy she was Jameson and I were finally together, we were out the door.

Jameson was quiet when we got in the truck, but I wasn't exactly a chatterbox either. I could hear my phone vibrating but ignored it. It started again as soon as it stopped. I fished it out of my bag and frowned at the unfamiliar number.

"Willa speaking," I answered.

"Honey, it's Lucy. Can you come down to the hospital?"

"Lucy? What's going on? Is everything okay?" My body had gone tight. Jameson noticed and reached over to touch my leg in silent support. Lucy practically lived at the police station. She was an institution, not just a receptionist. If she was at the hospital, something bad must have happened.

"It's best if you come here, and I'll tell you."

"No, tell me now. What happened?"

She must have heard the resolution in my voice because she gave in. "It's your dad. They brought him in an hour ago, and he's in surgery. I tried calling you earlier, but you weren't answering." That's because I was busy playing happy families with a family that wasn't my own. The guilt crashed over me and held on, clawing at my insides.

"I'll be there in ten."

"Okay, honey, I'll wait downstairs for you."

I hung up and turned to Jameson. "Can you take me to the hospital?"

"Of course. What happened?"

"Dad's there. I don't know what he did this time, but

he's in surgery." My voice broke, and I choked back a sob.

"Babe." One word that held more meaning than anything else. One word that told me he would be there for me. One word I treasured hearing from his lips.

We made it to the hospital in less than ten minutes. Jameson bent a few road rules along the way, something very much out of character for him, and dropped me off at the entrance. "Go inside. I'll park the truck and be there in a minute."

I nodded and jumped out. His voice stopped me from closing the door. "He'll be all right." He paused and smiled at me. "And so will you."

With his words swirling in my head, I rushed inside. Lucy met me in the lobby, her resigned expression not inspiring confidence. She took my hand and guided me to the waiting room and onto a chair. I followed meekly, too numb to protest. Lucy daintily perched on the edge of the chair next to me.

I swallowed the lump in my throat and found my voice. "Tell me what happened."

"Garret had a heart attack. They brought him straight in but had to perform emergency surgery."

I was expecting a bullet wound or a beating, but I never once considered the possibility of a heart attack. I nodded, my eyes wide, my thoughts going from guilt to worry and back to guilt again. I felt myself drifting, like a boat without a motor.

That's when an arm snaked around my shoulders and I was pulled into a familiar body. I didn't have to look up to know who it was. Jameson. My anchor.

Lucy's eyes went wide, and she looked Jameson up and down, not hiding her obvious delight. She winked at me, squeezed my hand, and got up. "I have to get back to the station. Call me if you need anything, honey."

I nodded again, the only movement my body would allow at that moment. Lucy's heels clicked on the floor on her way out, the sound echoing off the walls.

Jameson stayed next to me, offering his support any way he could. He read me well and knew I didn't want to talk. Instead of pushing me, he brought coffee and told me about the time Mason was shot in the ass while out hunting with his friends.

A nurse came in to get a few details, but Lucy had given her most of the information that she needed already, so the conversation was brief. Jameson was an unwavering presence by my side, his arm firmly around my shoulder, offering silent support.

After countless hours of sitting around and waiting, a tired-looking doctor dressed in scrubs walked into the waiting room.

"Willa Montgomery?"

I shot up and sprinted over, Jameson only a step behind me. "Is he okay?"

"I'm Doctor Caldwell. Your dad will be fine. We had to perform an angioplasty. What that means is that we widened the blocked areas with the help of a balloon to increase the blood flow to his heart. We also inserted stents to help keep his arteries open and reduce the chance of another attack. The operation went well, and he's in recovery but will be moved into a regular room soon. He needs to take it easy from now on and most of all change his diet."

That didn't surprise me since his diet consisted mostly of alcohol and cigarettes. Good luck trying to change him. I'd tried many times over the years to get him to stop destroying himself, but all attempts fell on deaf ears. And I was tired. So tired.

"When can I see him?" I asked, and Jameson squeezed my hand.

"As soon as he's in his room. I'll get the nurse to let you know once he's all set up."

"Thanks, Doctor."

He nodded at me, then Jameson, and left the room. I let out the breath I had been holding. Dad would be fine.

Jameson turned me to him, my front now pressed to his, two big arms creating a protective cocoon around me. "What can I do to make this easier?"

I wondered if anyone would notice if I ripped his pants off and gave him a blow job. He was just too perfect. But instead of risking arrest for indecent exposure, I said, "You're already doing it."

His hold tightened, and my arms snaked around his bulk. We stood there for a while, Jameson kissing my neck, and I burrowed closer. His gentle strokes calmed me and made me forget where I was. They also made my hands wander.

A throat clearing interrupted what would otherwise sure be known as the longest hug-turned-groping session. A nurse watched us with raised eyebrows. "Mr. Montgomery has now been transferred to his room. You can go see him if you want."

Jameson answered for me, since I seemed to have lost my voice. "We do. What's his room number?"

"Third floor, room 46." She walked off, leaving Jameson to lead us down the long corridor and into the elevator.

I hung my head, staring at the ground, holding back the tears and reminding myself that Dad was okay. I mindlessly followed Jameson, who never let go of my hand. We got out of the lift and went to Dad's room only to pause at the closed door. I was scared to open it. Maybe Jameson could distract me again.

"Do you want me to wait out here?" he asked.

There was no way I could make my feet move without him next to me. "No, I want you to come in. I mean, if you're okay with it. Of course you don't have to, but I'd love it if you did."

He kissed the side of my head. "Of course I'll come in."

He opened the door, and we walked inside. Since I was still gripping his hand in a death hold, I was forced to follow. It was either that or letting go, and there was no way I would release my lifeline.

Dad was propped up in bed, looking small amidst all the tubes and needles poking out of him. I inhaled sharply, not prepared for the view in front of me. He was always moving and talking, never one to stay still. The person in the bed looked nothing like him. He was pale and motionless.

"Dad," I said, my voice croaky from the tears I desperately tried to hold back.

He opened his eyes and blinked at me a few times. "Honey, what are you doing here?"

"What am I doing here? I'm here because you had a heart attack. I'm here because I'm your daughter. I'm here because I love you." Slight overreaction? Maybe. But my emotions were anything but contained.

"Honey, I'm fine. Just a little mishap."

"Right. A little mishap. Did they tell you what caused your little mishap?"

He looked away, embarrassment written all over his

face. "Sometimes these things just happen. You know how it is."

"I do know how it is. And when I talked to the doctor, he told me you need to change your diet and take it easy for a while."

"I will, honey. Nothing to worry about."

"Well, see, that's just it. I do worry. I worry about you all the time. I don't want to lose my dad because he's made one bad choice after another."

That seemed to make him think, but he didn't answer. Instead, he looked out the window, lost in his head. I knew that was as much conversation as I'd get out of him.

"I'm glad you're okay." I stepped closer to the bed and gave him a kiss on the cheek. "I'll be back tomorrow. You should try and get some sleep."

"All right, sweetheart. I will."

He turned his head away from me, and I knew I was being dismissed.

23

Jameson drove us back to his apartment. It was dawn, and I was dead on my feet. I needed a shower to wash the hospital smell off me. And a bed.

I stood in the bathroom, unsure of how I got there when Jameson came inside, carrying a towel. "I forgot to restock the bathroom." He set the towel down on the sink and walked up to me until we were almost touching. "Need some help?"

He pointed at the dress that I had pulled halfway up before I realized I needed to unzip it first. I hesitated a moment too long and he took it as an invitation. He pulled the zipper down, and then his hands skimmed over my shoulders, taking the fabric with them. He left the dress on the floor and pulled down my panties, then my bra.

I kept standing in the middle of the bathroom like a log, my mind blank, my body exhausted. He turned the water on and took his clothes off. Normally my eyes would be glued to his body. I would drink him in and hope I didn't miss an inch of his delectable form. But my vision was blurry, and I was unable to focus on anything.

Jameson led me into the shower and nudged me under the spray. The warm water was heaven to my tense muscles. When he began to shampoo my hair, I nearly melted into a puddle on the floor.

His fingers massaged my scalp with just the right amount of pressure. When he was done, he carefully rinsed me off and proceeded to put soap on every part of my body, his strokes slow and gentle. I sank into him, grateful that all I had to do was stand there. His hands lingered over my breasts, making sure to give them proper attention. I was ready to give in to anything as long as he kept touching me.

But instead of taking advantage of the situation, he nudged me back under the spray until there was no soap left. His hands continued to glide over my skin. I wished I wasn't so tired.

He kissed my shoulder before leading me out of the shower and wrapping a towel around me. Not the ending I expected, but the only one I could handle at the moment. He kissed me on the lips and rubbed his thumb over the spot he just kissed. "I left you one of my T-shirts on the bed. Go and sleep, babe."

He turned me around so I was facing the door and stepped back into the shower. I staggered out of the bathroom and managed to dry myself off half-heartedly and tugged the T-shirt over my head. I face planted on the bed and was out like a light.

When I slowly woke up, my eyes were heavy, my body not ready to move yet. I was too hot, my skin burning up. I tried to find my way out of the blankets but couldn't move.

And what was a girl to do but panic in a situation like this? My eyes shot open, my limbs started flailing, and my head smashed into something hard.

A loud groan sounded from behind me, and I realized I was in Jameson's bed, his big body half on top of me. I really needed to stop waking up like this.

"Babe, what are you doing?" His raspy voice stopped my jerky movements.

"I didn't know where I was and started panicking. Sorry for the headbutt."

He turned me around, so we were both on our sides, facing each other. One arm was still under my head, holding me in place and making a great pillow, and the other was under my shirt, drawing circles on my rib cage. "I'll live. Let's hope I won't get a shiner because that would be hard to explain."

I untangled my arm from the blankets and cupped his cheek. "I'll just tell everyone you defended my honor and sacrificed your pretty face in the process."

He huffed and tickled my side, making me squirm. "Pretty? You mean ruggedly handsome."

"Beautiful."

More tickling.

"Manly."

I tried to put some distance between us, but he was having none of it, holding me in place good and tight. "Cute."

"There is nothing cute about me, woman. I think it's time to remind you of my manliness."

He pulled the blankets over us and skirted down my body. I liked the direction this was going.

And he most definitely reminded me of how much of a man he was. Can't say I minded the way he showed me, either.

24

"You asked for three headlights, so I ordered three headlights. Before you say something you'll regret later, yes, I know a car only has two. I figured you might want extra just in case."

Mason ground his teeth, clearly trying not to stuff the rag he was holding into my mouth to shut me up. "Why would I order three fucking headlights? It's only one car. Doesn't make sense."

I was standing in Mason's car bay, and Landon was leaning against the hoist, enjoying the show. We were arguing about the latest shipment when a voice stopped me before I could really get into my tirade.

"No wonder you've forgotten all about your friends."

My head whipped around, and my sour expression turned into a huge smile. "Maisie!" I yelled and threw myself into her arms. "I thought we were meeting at the bar?"

We stood in a half embrace, and I looked her up and down to make sure the English hadn't stolen any of her limbs and stopped when I spotted her newest wardrobe addition. "I'm so going to borrow those shoes."

She winked at me. "If you're lucky."

I turned us around in the direction of the office and tugged her along with me. "I want to hear everything. Let's go to the office so there is no chance of any Neanderthals listening in."

My statement was met with a chorus of grunts and shouts. Neanderthal theory proven.

We escaped into the cool confines of my office, and Maisie looked around with interest. "Nice office." She walked behind my desk and pushed my desk chair out to sit down.

"No, don't sit—"

I was cut off by a loud squeak. Instead of sitting down, Maisie was sprawled on the floor, the chair pushed up against the wall. I rushed over to her and helped her get up. "Shit, are you hurt? I need to get the chair fixed. Two of the wheels broke off, and now it's a little unbalanced."

"How the hell do you break two wheels off?"

"Easy. Landon wouldn't leave the office and made himself at home in my chair. I pushed him out the door and the wheels got caught along the way and broke off." Maisie looked at me with doubt, and I threw up my hands. "He's heavier than he looks."

"Okay, spill it. Since when are you working at Drake's Garage and what the hell happened while I was gone?"

"Why don't we sit down for this conversation? Do you want coffee?" I dragged Maisie over to the couch and pushed her down. "I'll get us some coffee."

My beloved coffee machine didn't settle my nerves as

it usually did. The promise of caffeinated goodness was not enough to help me grow some balls and own up to all that had happened during the summer. Surely there was no need to tell her absolutely everything.

The familiar smell of freshly brewed coffee accompanied me on the way back to the office. Maisie was still where I left her, except she was sitting up straight, not hanging off to the side because some lunatic pushed her onto the couch.

"One sugar and a dash of caramel creamer. Clay ate all the cookies, and you probably guessed that there are definitely no cupcakes left."

Maisie laughed, throwing her head back, shaking her long locks. She didn't do things halfway, and she laughed often and loudly. It was infectious, and Stella and I were usually right there with her. Unless she laughed at the absence of cupcakes. One should never joke or laugh about missing cupcakes, hence why I cut her a stern look.

"So, how was London?" I asked.

Judging by the spark in Maisie's eyes, she wouldn't let me get away with my diversion tactics for long. "It was amazing. Saint Martins is an amazing fashion school. I had a class with Professor Wilson. She taught McQueen and Giles Deacon, can you believe it?"

As a matter of fact, I could, because I had no idea who any of those people were. "Does that mean you can make me my very own line now? And call it The Willa?"

"I didn't go over there to study architecture." Maisie was a bit touchy when it came to her fashion obsession. Stella and I had to walk over nails many times to get her to forgive us for teasing her.

"All I'm saying is to remember your friends when

you're rich and famous. The best way would be to name one of your lines after them, and invite us to your shows. Is that too much to ask?"

Maisie flipped me off, and I knew all was well again. "Of course you'll be invited. And I'll name my creations after you if you name your firstborn after me."

"Huh. Let's not be hasty."

"Enough about London. I want to know what's going on with you."

And I did tell her most parts, but I skimmed over the bits that included Jameson. And the part where I got arrested.

Now Maisie was staring at me and not in a good way. Not that there ever was a good way to stare at someone, but her way was disturbing. Eyes wide, mouth opening and closing, about to say something but then stopping herself.

"Do you need water? More coffee? Defibrillator?" I asked, ever the helpful friend.

I leaned over to touch her forehead. When I made a move to pinch her cheek, she intercepted my hand and swatted me away. "Still processing. That was some summer. Is your dad okay?"

"I spoke to the hospital this morning, and they want to keep him for a few days. Des brought him his clothes and checked up on him. Dad doesn't really want to talk to me right now." I lowered my head, and Maisie squeezed my hand.

"I can't believe you got arrested."

I covered my face with my hands and groaned loudly. "Don't remind me."

There was a knock on the door, and Landon came in. "Sorry to interrupt, ladies, but we need Willa to go through the orders with us. We don't want to end up with two left doors."

Jackass. You screw up once and they hold it over your head forever. And the headlight was totally Mason's fault. His writing was terrible and the number two looked like a three.

I checked my watch and noticed it was almost four. If we didn't get our orders in we wouldn't receive them the next day. "Shit, sorry, I'll come out now." I turned back to Maisie. "Give me ten minutes, and we can head over to Sparkie's."

"Can I come with you? I still can't believe you actually work here."

I was about to tell her no when Landon offered Maisie his arm with an obvious sweep of her body. "Of course you can, pretty lady. Shall we?"

I knocked my elbow into his side when I passed him and gave him my best angry Willa look, but since Landon was almost as big as Jameson, he didn't even flinch. And he flat-out ignored my crazy eyes.

I went out to the workshop, trying my hardest to ignore his flirting but couldn't help but make a gagging noise.

He retaliated by flicking my ear and went right back to his wooing. I had already started the orders earlier, so there wasn't much left.

Landon hadn't come up for air and talked nonstop as he walked Maisie out to the garage floor. I wasn't overly concerned since I knew he was as far from her type as he could get. She liked her men older, dressed in stuffy suits, and with a raised pinkie while they sipped on their overpriced whiskey.

The guys gave me the rest of their order, and I went to save Maisie from getting her leg humped.

"Maisie, I'm all done here. Let's go back to the office so I can place the orders and we can go."

She waved me off and continued to give her big eyed, "I'm so innocent" look to Landon. Oh puuuh-lease. I'd seen her blink her big brown eyes many a time. It was her best feature, as she liked to tell me often. I was getting annoyed. There was no need for her to lead him on only to drop him five seconds later.

I'd come to care for everyone here, and as much as I loved my best friend, I knew how she worked all too well.

"Maisie, come on." I gave her my best "let's go now or I'll slap you in your vajayjay" look, but she just ignored me.

An arm around my shoulders distracted me and halted Maisie's nonsensical dialogue faster than any of my feeble attempts.

"There you are. I missed you," a voice whispered in my ear.

I looked at Maisie who observed me with keen interest, and like the jerk I was, I stepped out of Jameson's reach, not acknowledging his greeting.

And then I made it worse by treating him like my boss, which technically he was. "Mr. Drake, do you have anything to add to the order?"

The guys gave me puzzled looks but otherwise stayed silent, which should have been the first indication of how badly I'd just screwed up. They never shut up. Never. I'd finally done the impossible and stunned them speechless.

I looked up and met Jameson's eyes but instantly wished I hadn't. The hurt passing over his features made me feel like a slimy slug dick. For lack of another option, I barged on, unable to undo what I had already broken.

"Have you met my friend, Maisie? Maisie, meet my boss, Mr. Drake."

Jameson's face showed disbelief that quickly morphed into anger, but I barged on like the bulldozer in a rose garden that I was. "We were just on our way out. See you tomorrow."

I snatched Maisie's arm and guided her back to the office, unable to meet Jameson's eyes or do more than wave a moronic goodbye at him. I was an idiot. An idiot who didn't want her friend to find out what she'd really been up to over the summer. Because Jameson had a reputation, and Maisie would not be happy about me becoming another notch on his bedpost.

"Don't think you'll get away with ignoring what just happened," Maisie whispered next to me.

"Later," I said, voice low to avoid making things worse.

Later turned out to be only thirty minutes, much to my horror. Stella met us at the bar, and Maisie wasted no time filling her in. "Willa had a busy summer. And she can't wait to tell us all about it."

I glared at Maisie. If I was being honest with myself, I wasn't really angry at her. She and Stella were my best friends. I would normally share every detail with them, but I had stuffed things up majorly. I shouldn't have been a coward and pretended Jameson and I weren't together in front of Maisie. God, I was an idiot, but I panicked. It was like my brain decided to be a fuckstick and make stupid decisions.

I took a deep breath. Still not ready, I took a long drink of my beer. The alcohol gave me the necessary courage, and I looked up, ready to face the Humptulips inquisition. No more stalling. "So I might have gotten close to Jameson this summer."

"You mean you got horizontal with Jameson this summer. And by the looks of it, that didn't just happen once," Maisie said. "He put his arm around you and whispered something in your ear. In front of everyone. You should have seen it, Stella. It was like the second coming of Christ."

She leaned closer to Stella and fake whispered, "They definitely got it on while we were gone."

They both inhaled loudly only to proceed to make a big O with their mouths. Bitches.

"Scandalous," Stella said. "Jameson doesn't do public anything, except stand there like a Greek statue." She seemed to mull it over. "Unless he's wasted. Because there was this one time at Maisie's party, and I remember him being lip locked with Regina—"

I put my hands up and yelled, "Stop it. I don't want to hear it. And in case you've forgotten, I was there."

And how could I forget that night. It was the night I fell into the pool. Now that might sound like a regular party occurrence, but it was winter and nipple-freezing cold. And the party was inside. I fell in because I was too busy spying on Jameson making out with Regina. I side-stepped and my foot met air after he met my eyes. Looked straight at me while Regina was making her way down his body. I panicked and forgot I was standing next to the pool.

Both Maisie and Stella started snickering with their hands held in front of their faces. As if that would stop the sounds from reaching me. They definitely remembered the incident. The only saving grace was my drowned state, which meant nobody recognized me straight away. Thankfully he was gone by the time I emerged from the bathroom dressed in Maisie's too tight clothes and more than a little humiliated.

"Which brings us to your tale of hot men," Maisie said.

I groaned and took another fortifying drink of my beer. "Well, you both already know that I work for him. And he's a pretty decent boss."

"And?" Stella probed.

"And he helped me pick Dad up from Vegas."

Both their faces snapped to attention. "He did what?" Maisie asked.

Stella leaned closer, putting her hand on my arm. "Be honest. Did you drug him?"

I pulled my arm back and narrowed my eyes. "I would never do that. He insisted on coming along. I didn't really have a choice in the matter."

They both nodded like I had just found the answer to removing wine stains without scrubbing. I felt like it was necessary to elaborate. "We are friends. We hang out after work. He was there for me when Dad had his heart attack."

More nodding.

"He's actually a pretty decent guy. And his family is lovely. Not like—"

"Whoa, hang on there, skippy," Stella said, both hands in the air, palms facing my way. "Did you just say you met his family?"

"Well, his brother works with him, so since I work there too and he went to our school, I already knew him. Technically I only met his mom."

"This is huge."

"Gigantic."

I didn't think of it that way before, but I did now. It must have meant something, surely. Because it's not every day you bring someone home. I was such an idiot.

"Shit. I totally screwed up."

"You sure did," Maisie said, ever so helpful.

She turned to Stella to fill her in on my screwup. "Our ignorant little friend here managed to turn a beautiful meeting of two soul mates into a bloodbath of love. You should have seen his face. It was heartbreaking."

Someone liked to lay it on thick. And they thought I was a drama queen.

"I pretended we weren't together because I didn't want you to judge me." That one was meant for Maisie who had made more than one scathing comment on Jameson and his long list of conquests. "And before you try to deny it, we all know how cutting your remarks can be, Maisie. Your opinion matters to me, and I wasn't sure how Jameson felt about everything. No need for a public service announcement when he was planning on dumping me by the end of the week anyway."

"Never seemed to have been his intention," Stella said.

Another long sip of my beer was in order. I had screwed up. "We know that now, not that it matters anymore. He looked hurt and incredibly angry." And I wasn't sure how forgiving he would be.

"He sure did," Maisie said. Not very encouraging, but at least she was honest.

"I think the only thing to do is to drown our sorrows and pray it will take out enough brain cells so I won't remember how badly I screwed up," I said.

"You should at least text him and say sorry," Stella said.

"Or send him a pic of your boobs." Maisie said, always helpful. "Your boobs are epic. All big and perky. Usually you get one or the other, but you won the boob lottery."

“I better give him some time to cool down first.” Like a year or two.

They both knew I’d reached my limit, and because we had been best friends for ages, both my girls dropped the topic and moved on to tales of London and Stella’s family’s farm. I loved them. They were the bestest friends a girl could have.

25

I HAD THE WORST FRIENDS. MY DRUNKENNESS LAST night hit unprecedented levels. I was too messy to be allowed in public, but they kept supplying me with drinks and encouraging words.

If I had great friends, they would have taken me home after I suggested doing a conga line through the Donut Hole, leaving a trail of ketchup and mustard in our wake. Instead, they joined in. Filthy traitors. And the worst part: they didn't even once think to take my phone away. What sort of friends wouldn't stop their nearest and dearest from texting whilst under the influence of one too many margaritas? Traitors. That's who.

Even though my texting was usually more a hit and miss of letters while drunk, I still somehow managed to get the messages out to the big wide world last night.

I woke up this morning with the mother of all hangovers and a serious case of texting regret. I stared at the trail of text messages from last night in horror. I prayed that Jameson hadn't read them. Maybe they got lost along the way. Sometimes messages didn't send. It happened all the time.

I scrolled back to the first text.

Me: *I love*

Me: *cupcakes*

Me: *I love cupcakes*

Me: *There's a direct causal link between my boob size and my fetish for cupcakes*

Me: *Stella tried giving me a Chinese burn. Turned into a Tongan burn*

Me: *Accidently typed Tongan tornado into Urban dictionary. I need to wash my eyes out with acid. Or margarita.*

Me: *Urban dictionary needs to list Tongan burn*

Me: *Tongan burn… your burn doesn't even touch the roof of the farm house*

Me: *I like big butts and I cannot lie they didn't accept my entry. Lame Dictionary*

Me: *That's meant to say I like big butts and I cannot lie*

Me: *NO ducking phone, I like big butts and I cannot lie*

Me: *Tell Landon to write his obituararary.*

Me: *After filixing my prune.*

Me: *I have three boobs.*

Me: *Long livet the cupacaaaaaake.*

He hadn't replied to any of my texts, and I doubted he would. Because who in their right mind would? They didn't make any sense.

My alarm went off again, telling me I was once again running late. Sorry, Rayna.

I took a shower, because nobody would appreciate eau de brewery, and ten minutes later I was on my way.

Since I had no car or bike, I had to take the bus. It took longer than anticipated, and I forgot to bring change. Apparently anything larger than a ten-dollar bill was unacceptable. I finally convinced the bus driver to take my money and keep the change. There went my food budget for the next two days.

After I missed my stop and had to walk the two miles back, I finally dragged my half-dead carcass into the bakery and slumped against the bench.

"What the hell happened to you? Did you miss out on Justin Bieber tickets again?" Rayna greeted me, already elbow deep in dough.

"Long night."

She winked at me. "Jameson must have some stamina."

I flinched like she had slapped me at her mention of Jameson. The flinch was too obvious, and she stopped kneading and turned all her attention to me. "Willa." One word and I was ashamed to admit I burst into tears. "Oh no, what happened? Come and rest your puddleface on your auntie's big chest."

I had to admit her boobs were right up there on the comfortable scale. Guess our family had good genes. I gladly accepted her invite and fell into her open arms. She held me tight and rubbed my back. Luckily, I had no aversion to dough. My back was sure to be covered in it.

It took me a while to pull myself back together and form a coherent sentence. Rayna waited me out like she always did, her presence comforting and warm.

I wiped my eyes and straightened up. Rayna's apron was now not only covered in dough but wet as well. It looked like she lost a round of doughwrestling.

"I screwed up."

"I figured."

"Hey, where's the support?"

She looked at my clothes, and I got the point. I was wearing a stained lime green T-shirt and purple pants. I couldn't recall ever buying them, but since I had missed laundry day for the fourth time in a row, I had to wear whatever didn't smell too bad.

I guess point made.

The day dragged on. Rayna let me eat whatever I wanted, which meant she knew how much I was hurting.

She usually cut me off after three pastries, but not today. Today I even got to sample the new chocolate cake she made. After I sufficiently stuffed myself, she handed me a bag of flour and pushed me in front of my bench space. "Now get to work. This stuff is not going to bake itself."

I swallowed the last of my red velvet cupcake and started measuring out ingredients. We worked in silence for a while until Rayna said, "You know you can still fix things with Jameson."

"I don't think so, Rayna."

"I saw the way he looked at you. It was more than passing interest."

"Didn't you listen when I told you how badly I screwed up?" I thought back to the look of betrayal on his face. I was such an idiot.

"Stop being such a drama queen and talk to him."

I hadn't yet told her about the text messages. Because before I sent them, I had every intention of talking to him. But now? Not so much. I'd barricade myself behind closed doors and hope he didn't need to speak to me when I went to the office later. I was embarrassed.

I stayed at the bakery for longer than usual. God knew I had a lot of hours to make up. I was also avoiding being by myself and without anything to do. Rayna shot me a few knowing looks but didn't say anything.

When I finally peeled myself away from Sweet Dreams, I was stuffed full of sugar and felt sick. The bus was slow, and it took me ages to get to the garage.

Jameson wasn't there when I got in, and the guys only shot me a few grunts in greeting. Guess Jameson wasn't the only one mad at me.

Nobody came into the office all afternoon. And I mean not a single person. No customer, no Landon, and no Jameson. I felt shittier than the waitress at Sparkie's who gets to unblock the toilets after they put their spicy buffalo wings on special.

I left without talking to anyone, feeling sorry for myself. Not only did I have a pounding headache, I also had a serious case of the regrets. So I did what I did best in situations that refused to solve themselves and ate a tub of ice cream and a few—read four—cupcakes for dinner.

It didn't make my world right again, but it certainly helped in my quest to finding my sugar limit. Everyone had one. That point where you know you've eaten way too much sugar-laden goodness and turn into a ball of useless energy only to crash a few short minutes later. I was grateful when I finally crashed.

26

This week was going to be officially the worst week in my tragically short life, because I had lost the will to live. It was official. I was unable to sleep, which caused me to be late for work every single day this week. Okay, I admit that wasn't really unusual, but I was later than ever before.

As a result, I would show up barely awake at the garage. Not that anyone would notice because the guys still weren't talking to me. They held a grudge better than Maisie and Stella did after finding out I bought myself four cupcakes and didn't share with them.

My car was still impounded. My bike was being held by the Humptulips Police Department as evidence. I forgot to pay my electricity bill and had been sitting in a dark apartment for the last few days.

The little fluffy monster from hell stole my vibrator again. This time I left him to it. He'd get more use out of it than I did. As mentioned before, I had lost my will to live, so no orgasms in my future. Because I wouldn't be on this earth for much longer.

And now it was Friday, and I was lying on my apartment floor with my feet up on the couch. The very same floor that I hadn't cleaned in a month. It was safe to say I'd be covered in crumbs and dust bunnies once I had the energy to emerge from my coma.

I tried drinking tequila but gave up after two shots. I really hated the stuff. But it was all I could find in my cupboards. I had even exhausted my secret stash.

Anything requiring me to leave my apartment was out of the question. I hadn't showered in two days. My last human interaction outside of Rayna, who was getting more and more impatient with my self-pity, was Dad. I picked him up from the hospital yesterday, borrowing Des's car.

He didn't say much and refused my help after I dropped him off at his trailer. I didn't argue for once and left him to it. He was a grown man. And I was a broken woman who was sure she was going to leave this earth for greener pastures soon. No need to leave more angry people behind.

So here I was lying on my filthy floor, waiting for death to take me. Only that death was being a lazy bitch and the floor was getting kind of uncomfortable. My inner rant was disturbed by my door opening. I didn't lock it, because what was the point? It would take a lot longer to find my body if they had to break the door down first.

"Depressed Daisy?"

"Loser face?"

Oh the love of two good friends was like a warm blanket on a cold winter's night. I had ignored all their messages. Because again, why drag things out? They would soon forget about me.

A face appeared above me. "Why are you lying on

the floor?" Maisie asked.

"It's disgusting in here. Do you ever open your windows?" This message of support came from Stella, who went straight to my windows and opened them, grunting at the effort. The frames were old and the latch a stubborn jerk. I just hoped I would be able to close them again since I wasn't done shutting out the world yet.

Maisie pulled on my leg. "Get your sad butt up off the floor and take a shower. We're taking you out."

"I don't want to."

More leg pulling ensued, much to my dismay. "Too bad, you're going." Maisie had her "don't fuck with me" face on. It had brought lesser women to their knees. Not me. I was standing at death's door already. A little intimidation would do nothing to me.

"I called O's. They're making their special pizza tonight, and they are saving you two servings of panna cotta."

Say no more. O's—Othello's if you wanted the actual name—was the best Italian food one could eat. It would make my perfect last supper. I shot up from the floor and sprinted to the bathroom.

"Did you book a table?" I called over my shoulder.

"Of course we did. What do you take us for? Amateurs?" Stella said, looking affronted.

I took the world's quickest shower, making sure to shave just in case I had an open casket. You never knew if it would be a dress they decided to put on me. A girl's gotta be prepared. No hairy legs for this corpse.

I came back into the living room and was met with two frowning faces. "You are not leaving the house dressed like that."

I looked down at my ensemble and didn't see

anything wrong with it. Jeans and T-shirts worked for anything. I was comfortable. And I planned on eating a lot, so I needed clothes that stretched. "What's wrong with my clothes?"

Maisie pulled me back into my bedroom, and Stella went to my closet. After sifting through the mess, she found a dress. Because I still hadn't gotten around to doing my laundry, a dress would be the only item still clean. I owned packets of new underwear to avoid having to go to the laundromat.

"Put this on," Maisie said, and Stella went to get my hairdryer and brush.

I crossed my arms in front of my chest and stepped back. "No way. That dress is bad news."

"Because you wore it to your date that ended with you pretending to go out with that waitress?" Stella asked, grinning.

"Yes. It's the dress's fault that my date was a misogynistic bastard. I'm not wearing it."

"Stop blaming innocent garments and put it on," Maisie said and turned to Stella. "What do you think, Stella?"

"Maisie," I said, putting as much warning in my voice as possible. She ignored me, and I stepped back again. It was time to cut my losses and run. I could mourn the loss of pizza later. I turned but didn't make it more than half a step.

Both Maisie and Stella tackled me to the ground. While Maisie pulled my T-shirt off, Stella made quick work of my pants.

Before I had time to regroup and tell them where to stick it, they slipped the dress over my head, sat me up, and zipped me in.

"Cute shoes," Stella gushed over a pair of black

heels I'd bought on sale three years ago but had never worn more than once. Turned out they were super uncomfortable. I got blisters just from standing up.

She didn't care about my yells for mercy and pushed them at me. "Put these on. They'll look gorgeous with your dress."

Maisie started on my hair, first brushing it out and then drying it. She produced a curling iron from her handbag and curled the shit out of my long mane. I shot the curling iron a look, and she shrugged. "I like to be prepared. Why do you think I carry a huge bag around with me?"

I was ready within thirty minutes. One look in the mirror confirmed my worst fears. I looked like Hollywood Barbie if she gained twenty pounds and wore midnight blue vintage dresses.

My long mane was perfectly curled around my face, and my flawless makeup, courtesy of Stella, made me look alive, hiding the dark circles under my eyes. Instead they were artfully made up with earthy tones, enhancing the green sprinkle around my irises.

They both stood in front of my front door, blocking it. Maisie snapped her fingers at me to stop me from looking at my reflection in the hallway mirror. "Say it."

I rolled my eyes. "Fine. Thanks, Maisie and Stella. You did a great job, and I really need to get out of the house." Everyone needed one last hurrah after all.

Maisie put an arm around me and pulled me into a half hug. "Now, that wasn't so hard, was it?"

Stella took my hand, and together we made our way outside and into a taxi. O's was only a short ride away, not that anything was more than a thirty-minute car ride in our small town. Things just seemed impossibly far away if you had to go the distance on a bike or the bus.

Lulu greeted us when we entered, cheery as ever. "My doves have returned. I have a special table reserved for you." She always had a special table for us. She said that to every customer. But we loved her and the food and wouldn't complain if she decided to seat us outside during a snow storm.

"This is nice. Us girls catching up. Having a great time," Maisie said after we had been sitting in silence for a while. I was such a downer, I couldn't even stand my own company right now.

I shouldn't leave this world on a bad note, so I had a brilliant idea. "Let's do shots." The only way to leave this earth was with more bad decisions and embarrassing dance moves.

"I'm in," Stella said, throwing a fist up in the air.

Maisie's eyes lit up. "Me, too."

Well that was easy. I waved to Juan, Lulu's nephew, and he sauntered over. He was shorter than me and smaller than all of us but had more energy and personality than anyone I knew. In short, he was hilarious.

"Gorgeous ladies, what can I get for you?"

"A bottle of limoncello and three shot glasses please," I said.

He grinned at us and winked. "I see you're ready to finally try the good stuff. Bottle of Lulu's homemade limoncello is coming right up."

The stuff was lethal. It tasted like fresh lemons and summer but hit you like a falling coconut that you were too slow to avoid. Our saving grace was dinner. Carb heaven that helped soak up the alcohol.

I wasn't usually a big drinker but extenuating

circumstances this week called for it. And of course, the fact that it was my last night on earth. My heart would soon give out, not only from the permanent squeeze it seemed to suffer from since Jameson left—or since I hurt him so badly he refused to talk to me—but also from all the crap I decided to stuff into my body.

To say we were merry once we finished dinner would be an understatement. At least I wasn't thinking about Jameson anymore but instead was concentrating hard on putting one foot in front of the other and not throwing up all over my shoes.

We stumbled out of O's and shuffled the two blocks down to O'Malley's. After two toilet breaks and one lost —and found again—shoe, we crashed through the door of the pub, giggling and drawing more attention than required when you're already well on your way to making a fool out of yourself. The only saving grace: it was Friday and the pub was packed with the after-work crowd. We'd hardly stick out unless Stella continued to take off her clothes.

Maisie wasted no time in spotting her target for the night and left me and Stella behind in the dust. The crowd was a mix of blue-collar workers, suits, and college students. And that's what made O'Malley's a great night out every time. You never knew how the night would turn out.

Stella and I ordered water from the bar, both having decided we would rather avoid a close encounter with the disgusting pub toilets. My stomach had settled, but one more sip of anything alcoholic would tip me over the edge.

I let my eyes travel the bar, content to just sit down and take it all in. I was almost reaching a state one would call close to contentment when my eyes fell on Landon, Mason and Clay. They looked happy, joking around while a few girls hung around them, waiting for whatever attention the guys would bestow upon them. My drunk brain could only come up with: How dare they have fun without me?

I didn't know when I made the decision to get up, but I was halfway across the crowded room before I realized the direction I was moving in. But I continued because in for a penny and all.

I stopped in front of their table, hands on my hips, lips pursed, ready to lay into them.

"Look who decided we are worthy of her attention," Landon said.

His comment made me fluster my ruffled feathers. "You mean you are offended that I didn't come crawling up to you and beg for your forgiveness? After you ignored me all week?"

"I wasn't the one embarrassed about my boyfriend."

"Embarrassed? Embarrassed? *Embarrassed*?" Okay, things were taking a turn for the worse. I couldn't seem to stop saying the same word over and over again, my voice getting higher with each word. Heart, now would be a good time to stop beating, because if I kept going on my current course, my headstone would read "In memory of Willa, who died when her head exploded."

"We might not have gone to some fancy college, but we know when someone doesn't want to be seen with us."

Holy shit, they all looked hurt over my Jameson snub. When did this turn into a group action, instead of a lover's quarrel? Yup, I said it. Quarrel. It's a thing. And sounded much better than describing the incident as *the time I pretended Jameson was nothing more than my boss because I didn't want my friend to know that we were sexing it up even though I love him.*

"That had nothing to do with you."

"It has everything to do with us. He is our fearless leader. We stick together. And you clearly have a problem about what he does. Good enough to have fun with behind closed doors but not to be seen in public, especially not with your friends around."

I never in a million years would have thought that this is what they would think about me. The anger was bubbling to the surface, and I was ready to punch the arrogant bastard right where it hurt.

"You are wrong. There isn't any way to explain this to you other than fuck you, that's not what I was doing at all." That's me, always mature and taking the high road.

Landon leaned back in the booth and glared at me. "Then explain to me what you were doing, your highness."

Oh no, keep it together, Willa. If you start a fight they'll kick you out. And Landon was double my size. One flick of his finger, and I'd be sprawled on the floor. Not that I thought he would ever hurt me.

Those were my last rational thoughts before rhyme and reason left the building, allowing crazy and loud to enter instead.

"I don't know what I was doing, okay? It was a dick move, and I know it. I regretted it the second it happened, but it had nothing to do with you guys or where you come from." I waved my hands around the now silent table. Every eye was on me.

I forged on, because at this stage I had nothing left to lose. "I'm in love with him." Oh God, did I just admit that out loud? Never will I drink a drop of the evil truth serum, aka limoncello, again. "I didn't mean to act like I was better than him or you guys. Now stop being such a fucking dipstick and talk to me like you used to. With lots of bad words. And condescending gestures. And then you usually hug me."

A hand on my arm stopped my rant. Stella had finally shoved her way through the crowds. I was grateful because a graceful exit was not an option at this stage. I could only hope I could slink away without causing more damage.

"It sure was a dick move." Landon got up and stood in front of me. "Swear on your aunt's red velvet cupcakes that you'll never do it again."

I suppressed the eye roll that threatened to break out for its moment of fame and said, "I swear on my aunt's red velvet cupcakes and double choc brownies that I'll never do it again."

And with just those words, all anger left his face and he pulled me into a tight hug. "I forgive you. But that means you are our cupcake bitch for the next two weeks."

Damn it, I knew what that meant. I had to bring cupcakes every single day. But it was fucking worth it because as soon as I made my amends with Landon, all the guys seemed to relax and stop throwing me daggers. "Fine. But I choose the flavor."

"I have no problem with that." He looked to Stella who was silently standing next to me. "Who's this? Another friend you'll show how much you don't like us?"

I stepped on his foot and leaned all my weight on it. "Don't push it, buddy."

I introduced them and watched in fascination as

another one of my friends fell victim to Landon's dimples and overused lines. Unbelievable.

"As much fun as this uncomfortable conversation was, we better get going," I said to Landon and turned around. Unfortunately, my eyes fell on Jameson like he was the red velvet cupcake in a sea of boring vanilla ones.

He was heading our way with none other than Regina trailing after him. Seeing him brought back every single feeling I had locked up tight. He might as well have slapped me over the head with a wrench; it would have hurt less than seeing him with someone else.

He was listening to Regina and thankfully hadn't spotted me yet. Panicked, I turned to the guys. "Seeyou-Mondaygottagobye." It all came out as one word in my rush to get the hell out of the bar.

I turned around and barely avoided a near collision. They must have been closer than my blurry vision led me to believe. Kill me now. Or make me invisible. I couldn't do this. I had to get out. Fast. Because this could not be happening right now. I wasn't ready. I hadn't even rehearsed my speech yet. It was only half finished.

I stared at Jameson who was now looking at me, ignoring whatever Regina was babbling on about. Probably her new car. Or her dog, the vicious little shit. Never trust a dog that fits into your handbag is my motto.

I looked at her perfect hair, her perfect dress, her perfect figure and felt perfectly inadequate. I had to get out. Of course my brain chose that moment to short circuit, and I blurted, "I quit."

Jameson stepped closer, his face drawn tight. "No,

you fucking don't." His voice was so low I could barely hear him.

"I can do whatever I damn well please. And right now quitting pleases me greatly."

He closed the distance between us, seriously invading my personal space. Oh dear, not good. Not good at all. Because the closer he was the more my nerve endings sparked alive, demanding my body to throw itself at him. *Down body, down. You are meant to be taking your last breath soon. Not coming back to life.*

"Well, I don't accept your resignation." I could tell he was still trying to hold on to his iron control, but his voice rose at the last word.

Time to get my ass out of here or risk making a scene. "I'm not doing this with you in a crowded bar." This was embarrassing enough without an audience.

Regina watched us with way too much interest and a smug look on her face. Gah, I hated her. Everyone would know about Jameson breaking up with me in about two point five seconds. She had some nimble texting fingers, that one.

I took Stella's hand and pulled her closer to get ready for our escape. I moved to step past Jameson, but he stopped me. Oh holy donut gods please make me keep my hands next to my body and stop me from touching anyone inappropriately. And by anyone I meant Jameson.

"You're not quitting your job."

I ignored him and instead glared at Regina who was standing entirely too close. It might have been more a one-eyed stare, but who cared at that moment. "Guess you got what you wanted from me and moved on," I said, unable to keep the words in.

I watched the vein in his neck start to pulse. Right,

time to step back slowly. Don't want to set him off. No sudden movements. I held it together until he reached out and pulled me closer, his hands on my arms.

I would not be held responsible for any and all of my actions from now on. Because touching was involved. His hands were on my body. This shouldn't be such a big deal. He'd touched me a lot over the last few weeks. Yet at this moment, it was.

I was forced to let go of Stella when he pulled me forward. There was my lifeline gone.

He bent down and spoke next to my ear, so that only I could hear him. "I thought you'd realize how fucking ridiculous this is and come to your senses. But I can see now that you are more stubborn than I thought. So let me tell you what you're going to do. You are going to walk out of this bar with me, and I'm driving you home. Whatever you think is going on here isn't happening."

"Don't tell me what to do," I said.

"This isn't a choice," he said, his anger replaced with exasperation.

He turned to Stella. "Are you okay to get a ride home?"

She nodded, the traitorous traitor, and pointed to the bar. "Maisie is here as well. I'll share a cab with her."

Jameson nodded, and without so much as a glance at Regina, he held me close and pushed through the crowd. I resisted the urge to flip her off on my way out. Mammoth effort.

He didn't release his hold on me until we were at his truck. Ever the gentleman, he helped me inside and buckled me in. He didn't say a word the whole way back to my apartment; I officially had the Neanderthal version of Jameson back.

The short ride didn't help my drunk mind make any sense of the situation. I also couldn't come up with an excuse, because I wanted to tell him how sorry I was. How stupid and insecure.

We got out of the truck, but instead of letting him help me out, I dragged my uncoordinated self out before he had a chance to come around to my side. He wordlessly took my key and pushed the door to my apartment complex open. The bitch didn't even so much as creak but swung open effortlessly instead.

I followed him up the stairs, staring at his back. I knew I had irreparably damaged whatever relationship we had because he didn't even walk behind me but made me follow him. And he always walked behind me to make sure I was okay. And look at my butt. It was one of the many things I loved about him. And there, I said it. I wasn't just in like. I was in love and didn't even get to say the words to him before I fucked it all up.

We arrived at my door, and Jameson once again took over opening the door. Even in my drunk state I could admit it would have taken me a few tries to get the key in. I knew my limits and had gotten well past them again tonight. But that was okay since it was my last hurrah after all.

He didn't come inside but instead handed me my key. "I'll see you tomorrow, okay? Try and get some sleep."

I didn't move inside but instead turned to face him. "I'm so sorry. I wish I could take back what I did." My voice was hoarse, my heart torn, and to top it all off, I felt a tear escape. I was such a gigantic idiot. A drunk gigantic idiot who was now a crying idiot.

I hoped I wouldn't remember this tomorrow. Maybe I'd forget I even saw Jameson. Not interested in humiliating myself further, I finally turned around to close the door.

Instead of closing it, the damn thing opened all the way and Jameson was in front of me. "Fuck. Willa. I can't—" He didn't finish his sentence but instead curled his big body around me and held me tight. I cried for a while, and I wasn't proud to admit it, but it lasted this long because I knew he'd let me go once I stopped, not because I felt like crying anymore. Even I couldn't keep the tears going after he stroked my hair and back and whispered nonsense in my ear. I buried my nose into his shirt and inhaled deeply. This would have to last me for a while.

Instead of releasing me, he pulled me closer. "Do you remember Maisie's party? The one where you fell in the pool?"

Huh? What did that have to do with anything?

"Yeah?" I croaked out.

"That was the night I knew that you were it for me. I'd seen you around school but didn't pay much attention. You were a few grades below me, and I was about to graduate. But that night I saw you and my whole world turned upside down."

"What?" My voice was strangled, the emotions crashing in all around me. Did he just say that we had been a few years in the making? Because Maisie's party was five years ago.

"But you were with Regina."

"We broke up that night. I was going to find you the next day, but when I got to school, you were making out with Colton behind the bleachers."

I had no words. This was crazy. My heart threatened to jump out of my chest. "We were dating."

He lowered his head until we were forehead to forehead. "I know. That's why I backed off. And then the whole thing with Hannah happened and I ended up moving to Seattle."

I remembered him leaving. It was a dark day for the female population of Humptulips but a golden opportunity for Jameson. His friend Granger ran one of the most famous and successful garages in the country. Jameson did his apprenticeship there and came back to open Drake's with his brother.

"I know you are not ready to hear this, but I need to say it. I love you. I love you so much that the thought of losing you tears me in half. I hate that you think you have to hide us, that you don't trust me."

It was in that moment that I knew. Knew without a doubt that I felt the same. But the words wouldn't come. I stayed mute, my breaths coming loud and quick.

Jameson pulled back. "Go get some rest. We'll talk tomorrow."

What? He just told me he loved me, had at least liked me for the past five years, and now he was leaving? I blinked hard to clear my fuzzy brain, but it wasn't working. When I didn't move, Jameson took my hand and led me to my bed. *Now that's more where I thought this was going.*

He pulled my dress over my head and yanked the covers back. "Sit down, babe."

Wasn't going to argue, that's for sure. He took my shoes off, got a T-shirt out of my dresser, and pulled it over my head. Okay, now this wasn't where I thought this was going.

When he nudged me back until I was lying down and then kissed my head, I knew this was definitely not going where I thought it was.

"Sleep. I'll see you tomorrow."

I didn't get a chance to protest, and the last sign of Jameson was the door closing behind him. Maybe my tired old body might have a few years left of life after all.

My reason for breathing was back. At least I thought it was. Because he did say that I'd see him tomorrow.

That was my last rational thought before I passed out.

27

Maybe my body wasn't ready to live again after all, because at the moment I sure felt like I was dying. What happened last night? Did I try and kill myself with tequila? And who put cotton balls in my mouth?

A stretch of my arms confirmed I was alone in bed. Okay, that was good. So things didn't get too out of hand. I opened my eyes and looked at a familiar ceiling. I was at home. Even better.

Now if my face wouldn't be so numb and the rest of my body so achy, life would almost be normal again. I retraced my steps last night and remembered everything pretty clearly until we left O's. Damn limoncello. Guess I wasn't trying to end my life with tequila but with the lemony goodness instead.

My phone was blinking at me wildly from my nightstand. I did not remember putting it there, but at least I hadn't lost it again. With a loud groan, I rolled onto my side and lifted my arms to pick it up.

The first message was from Maisie.

Maisie: *I can't believe you left with Jameson without telling me. You better call me as soon as you wake up.*

And it all came back to me. Jameson driving me home. My breakdown. Him telling me he loved me. And then tucking me into bed.

I had to call him. Or would it be too soon? Maybe I should wait until tonight. Or tomorrow. Maybe he changed his mind. What if he did? After all, he didn't stay.

The next message was from Stella.

Stella: *Made it home okay. Maisie is pissed she missed the Jameson drama. Meet at Sweet Dreams for coffee when you wake up?*

Coffee. That's what I needed. I just didn't know if I could make it all the way to Sweet Dreams.

There was also a message from Des.

Des: *I heard what happened with you and Garret. You did the right thing. Come over if you wanna talk.*

I wasn't ready to talk to him yet but was sure that without a hangover I would be more willing to make amends. But first I needed a shower. I smelled of limoncello and meatballs, a dangerous combination if you're one sniff away from throwing up last night's dinner.

After I dragged my body into the shower and stood in the weak trickle until it turned cold, I felt a little more human. I shuffled into the kitchen in one of Jameson's T-shirts that might have fallen in my bag at one stage and big wool socks. Putting on pants was too much of an undertaking.

My next stop was the coffee machine. The coffee tin felt suspiciously empty, and once I opened it my worst fears were confirmed. I was out of coffee. Didn't even have the disgusting instant stuff left.

A knock at the door pulled me out of mourning. I was slumped over the counter and still thinking about whether or not I should go and let whoever was out there in when it opened. I had given a key to only one person besides my dad.

"Are you still alive? And decent?" Maisie called out, the loud noise making my head pound.

Her shoes clacked loudly on the floor, causing me to bury my head in my hands, still half lying on my kitchen counter.

"Go away."

"Where is Jameson?"

"Not here."

"Why?"

I lifted my head to glare at her. "How would I know? He dropped me off, told me he loved me, and left."

"He what?" Maisie's voice was too loud. Why was she here?

"Left. Now can I feel sorry for myself in peace?"

She clacked her tongue at me and pulled me upright. "Put on some pants. I'm not watching you like this any longer. You love him. He loves you. Let's go and tell him."

"How do you know I didn't say it back last night?"

She let go of me, and I sagged back onto the counter, this time leaning on it. Maisie crossed her arms and raised her brows. "Really?"

"Fine. I didn't say it back, but I can't go anywhere. I'm not feeling well."

This time she rolled her eyes and came closer. "Get dressed. If you don't, I'll drag you out of here dressed in what looks like Jameson's shirt. You have two minutes."

I grumbled in response but did go and put on some pants and change the shirt. Maybe I could convince her to stop at a coffee shop.

We got into her car and stopped at the coffee shop

with only one threat of bodily harm on my part and more than one eye roll on Maisie's.

Once the caffeine was coursing through my system, I felt better. I could totally talk to Jameson. He wouldn't have changed his mind overnight, and I was ready to do some groveling.

We pulled up to the garage, and I sank deeper into the seat, wondering if it was too late to turn around and go back home again.

A slap to my thigh made me shriek and sit up again. "What the hell, Maisie? What was that for?"

"For you being such a chickenshit." Her expression turned somber, and she turned in her seat to face me. "Look, I'm sorry for talking shit about Jameson and for judging him without even knowing anything about him. He seems like a great guy, and I was wrong."

"Oh my God, am I dying?"

She slapped me again. "Shut up. I can apologize when it's necessary. I've just never done anything before that warranted an apology. I'm basically perfect. Now will you close your mouth and get your ass in there so I can stop feeling guilty?"

I nodded and got out of the car. If Maisie of all people could admit that she was wrong, then I could do it, too. Determined to tell Jameson that I was an idiot, I walked into the garage.

"Sweetcheeks. You're either running really late or you're looking for Jameson," Landon said, knowing full well why I was there on my day off.

"What do you think?"

"Jameson."

"Correct. Is he here?"

"Sure is. But not sure if you want to get any closer. He's in a mood."

I could guess why and hoped he would want to see me.

Despite Landon's warning, I walked over to Jameson's bay. He was halfway underneath a car and didn't see me approach. I stood in front of his feet awkwardly, not sure what to say. I cleared my throat. "Jameson?"

He pushed himself out but stayed on the floor. I looked down at him, suddenly tongue tied.

"Willa. What are you doing here?"

"I just wanted to tell you that—" My voice broke and I backtracked. Because I most definitely was a chickenshit. "—Landon broke the fridge door."

"You traitor," Landon called out and took off.

Jameson watched me but didn't react to my news. "Right. And you came all the way over here on your day off to tell me that?"

"Yes. I mean no. There was something else."

He stood up, standing close, but didn't touch me. He wasn't going to make this easy for me. Guess I deserved that.

"I also wanted to apologize." I forced myself to look at him. "I'm sorry for what I said. I didn't mean it. If I could take it all back, I would. Being with you meant more to me than I ever realized. Life sucks without you. I kinda got used to having you around. And I also kinda like you. A lot."

"So you got used to having me around."

I nodded. That wasn't an altogether terrible speech. I had done worse. But why did he not look convinced?

"And you also kinda like me."

I nodded again. Not sure my fumbled words were having the desired effect. He wasn't exactly looking ready to forgive me. I guess I hurt him worse than I thought.

Unable to stay there any longer, I turned on my heels and walked outside. I could try something different. Maybe I'd write him a letter. At least that way I could think about what I wanted to say. Maisie was waiting for me outside her car, her forehead creased with worry. I was halfway through the parking lot when her eyes went wide. My steps faltered, and I was suddenly airborne.

"What the hell?"

"Where do you think you're going?" Jameson asked.

"Well, home most likely."

"I don't think so. Didn't you know the best part of having a fight is the make-up sex?"

My grin was so big it threatened to split my face in half. "Does this mean you forgive me?"

"Only if there is something else you want to tell me?"

He set me back on my feet, and I turned around and threw myself into his arms, wrapping myself around him until there was no space left between us. "I love you," I said into his neck. It was muffled, but he could make out the words since he hugged me tight and kissed the top of my head.

"I know. I just wanted to hear you say it."

I tipped my head back, and Jameson bent down and his lips met mine. I was home. I was happy. And I had the other half of my heart back.

EPILOGUE

"Mmmbldmm."

"Babe, wake up, your phone is ringing."

"Mmmmmmgggddl."

I was pushed into the mattress by a big body. Something I wasn't opposed to at all until the big body started talking. "Hello?"

I refused to open my eyes but could make out a voice on the other end of the line. Jameson answered with a few grunts here and there and finished the call.

A hand brushed my hair back, and I snuggled closer. "Willa, that was your uncle. Your dad wants to see you."

My eyes shot open, and I blinked at Jameson, who was suspended above me. I tried to get up, but he didn't move. "Des said he's fine. He's going through therapy, and they want family members to come up for a therapy session with him."

Dad had agreed to go to rehab four weeks ago. I hadn't seen him since he left because he didn't want anyone to visit. I was nervous, so I asked, "Will you come with me?"

"Of course. I'll do whatever you need me to do." He

turned us over, so I was lying on top of him. I nodded into his neck and sank into him, relaxing. I'd pretty much moved into his apartment. Most of my clothes were here, and I had spent exactly zero nights at my place over the last few weeks.

"What time do you have to be at the bakery?"

Shit, not again. "What time is it?"

Jameson handed me my phone. "Noooo, it's almost eight. I was supposed to be there ages ago." I scrambled off Jameson, kneeing him in the stomach on my way to the floor. "Why didn't my alarm go off?"

I was on all fours, scrambling for my clothes, finding my jeans but not my panties. I guess I could go without. Jameson had followed me off the bed, still naked and seemingly unaffected by the crazy person that seemed to have taken over my body.

I raced past him, but he caught me with an arm around my waist. "I'll drive you."

I kissed his chin, all I could reach if he didn't bend down to meet me halfway, and went into the bathroom to at least brush my hair and teeth. A girl's gotta have some standards.

When I came back out, he was fully dressed and in the kitchen. And was that coffee I smelled? Be still my beating heart.

Jameson pulled out a travel mug and filled it with freshly brewed coffee. I sighed in delight and blurted out, "Oh God, I love you. We definitely should get married."

I could probably blame it on withdrawal symptoms. Yup, that's what I was going with. Jameson held the cup out of my reach, his eyes fixed on me. "Say it again."

"Say what again?"

"You know what."

"I didn't say anything."

"Willa." Alrighty then, he was clearly not buying it. I sighed. I fidgeted. And I relented. It was time to put on my big girl panties. Even though I wasn't currently wearing any because I couldn't find them.

"Fine. I love you and may have blurted that I want to marry you. Now can I have my coffee?"

He handed it to me and crushed me and my coffee cup to his chest before I had a chance to take a sip. "I love you, too. And the answer is yes."

I never got enough of hearing him say it. Since he first said the three words, he'd repeated them all the time. They had become the three most important words in my life. Up until today, I had been too much of a coward to say them back.

"The answer to what?"

"You proposing to me."

"I wasn't proposing."

"Sure sounded like you were to me. Did you not just say we should get married? Not the most romantic proposal, but I'll take it."

He was grinning down at me, and I bit my bottom lip instead of answering. We had never talked about it, but I was totally down with marrying him. In a few years.

"Well, now that's cleared up, we should probably get going," I said, trying to lighten the suddenly serious mood.

He shook his head and planted a light kiss on my lips.

"Right. You got everything?"

I nodded, holding up my bag to prove I remembered to take it with me. He took my hand and walked me out to his truck, opening the door before going around to the driver's side.

"I'll pick you up after work and take you to see your dad. They said you can drop in from midday onward. And don't think you can just change your mind about the whole marriage thing. We are now as good as engaged."

I did a little happy dance inside because Jameson was it for me. And apparently he felt the same way. It didn't matter when we would make it official, all that mattered was that he was my person and I was his.

Thank you so much for reading Some Call It Love. The series continues with Stella and Mason's story. Read on for an excerpt.

If you enjoyed this book, please consider leaving a review. They help other readers discover my stories and are the fuel that keeps authors going.

Don't forget to sign up to my newsletter for news on upcoming books and for a newsletter exclusive novella (set in the Sweet Dreams series world).

SOME CALL IT TEMPTATION

CHAPTER 1

"That's not the right hole. You have to stick it in here."

"I know where to put it in. Go away and let the professionals do their jobs."

"And I'm not a professional?"

"Not when you wave that thing at me. It stinks."

I watched Landon, one of the mechanics, and Mason, one of the owners of Drake's Garage, argue from where I was standing in the doorway. Their heads were under the hood of an old car that looked ready to go to the junkyard, and they were bickering while Landon was eating a giant sandwich.

I worked at Drake's while their receptionist Willa was traveling around Europe with her boyfriend, Jameson, the other owner of the garage and Mason's brother. Willa was one of my best friends, and when she found out that I didn't have a job lined up after I finished college, she asked if I could help out while she was away.

Since I needed the money and there wasn't anything I wouldn't do for her, I agreed. I was desperate to get out of my hometown, Humptulips, and to be able to do that, I needed to save up some money. The small, sleepy town was in the middle of nowhere, and if I wanted to get out from under my mother's thumb, my only option was to move away. Not only had Willa organized a job for me, she also let me stay at her apartment rent free for as long as I needed.

When they stopped arguing to take breaths, I seized the opportunity to call out to them, "Carter is on the phone. He wants to speak to Mason."

I heard a loud groan, followed by a bang, and then Mason's head came up from underneath the hood.

"Can't you handle it?" he muttered. "I'm never doing a favor for Willa again."

There went my hard-won equilibrium. "You're doing her a favor? Don't you mean I'm doing you a favor by helping out while she's travelling?"

He brushed me off and went inside the office. "We could have hired someone from the temp agency."

I followed him and stood on the opposite side of the desk. It was always a good idea to put space between me and Mason. Things happened when we were standing too close. Confusing things.

"You mean the temp agency that blocked your number?"

He grumbled something unintelligible under his breath and picked up the receiver. After talking to Carter for all of five seconds, he hung up, then aimed another glare at me and stalked out.

I rolled my eyes at the closed door and got back to work. His annoyance at my presence wasn't anything new. And I'd learned to just ignore it. For the most part.

The day was busy, the garage popular, and I lost track of time. I was entering numbers into a spreadsheet when I felt someone watching me. Judging by the raised hairs on my arm and the warmth I felt in my belly, it could only be one person.

"Is there a reason why you're back already?" I asked, my voice sugary sweet. No point poking the bear unnecessarily.

"I need more oil filters for the Bronco," Mason said, his stare game going strong today.

I nodded. "Okay."

"Why aren't you writing this down?" he asked, the deep timbre of his voice resonating through my body.

"Because I'll be able to remember oil filters."

Despite what he thought, I wasn't an idiot. But try telling him that. He seemed to have cast his judgment already.

"I also need brake pads for the Mustang."

I forced a smile on my face. "No problem. Anything else?"

"Spark plugs for the Audi."

"You got it."

"You're still not writing anything down. How do you know how many to order for each?"

I fought the eye roll and won. "That's three items. And Willa wrote down how many to order of each before she left. I think I can remember three things." I sighed.

"Can you, though?"

I ignored his jab and smiled at him sweetly. I had perfected putting a mask in place when I needed to, and good manners had been drilled into me from birth. "Anything else?"

"I need it by tomorrow."

"No problem."

"Means you need to send the order now."

Not sure how much longer I could hold back that

eye roll that was desperate to come out. "I can handle it. Now can I get back to work?"

He didn't say anything else, just glared at me with his beautiful emerald eyes—that were totally wasted on the jerky shithead—and left the office. Good riddance. There was only so much time someone could spend staring at all the gloriousness that was Mason Drake. Too bad he was such a butt wipe.

One that had the nicest arms I had ever seen. They were muscular and defined. And I've always had a weakness for toned arms. They were my kryptonite. Fortunately, he didn't know that. Unfortunately, he liked to wear tight T-shirts that showed me entirely too much.

I made myself another cup of instant coffee—the only thing available since I broke the coffee machine on my second day at the office—and ordered the parts His Majesty requested.

The day went by in a blur, and I was still in the office an hour after closing. Willa told me I could leave as soon as I turned the Closed sign on the door. Technically that was true. But since the computer wasn't working properly, everything took forever, and I had a few invoices I needed to pay.

Tonight was one of the nights I usually babysat for my friend Nora, and I only had thirty minutes to get home. Lucky for me, peak-hour traffic wasn't a thing in Humptulips. I would have time to finish answering the last email that was titled urgent, then could rush home and still make it.

The workshop was busy, and the guys usually worked long hours, so there were still plenty of people around.

Landon came inside as I was packing up. "What are

you still doing here?" he asked and stopped at the door with his brows raised.

"I'm on my way out, just had to finish up a few things."

"Pretty much anything can wait until tomorrow. You don't have to work late, you know."

I liked to do a good job and that meant getting my work done. Despite what most people thought about me, I was not a ditzy idiot. I got a scholarship to college and I studied hard.

None of the things I accomplished in my life were because of who my family was. The Connors were notorious in Humptulips; my mother owned a huge cattle ranch and half the businesses in town. Everyone thought I had it all, but nobody really knew how oppressive a life I had led.

I shouldered my bag and gave him a half-smile, which was all I had in me at the moment. "Didn't want to mess up on my first day. The computer wasn't working properly, so it took a bit longer. But I got it done."

He nodded and walked closer. "If you ever need anything, come and find me."

I guessed him to be around my age, and he had the boy-next-door look perfected. His light green eyes and curly dark brown hair would make many a woman sigh in delight. Something I knew for a fact since I'd seen him in action.

I made my way to the door. "Thanks, that's a really nice offer. I will."

The door to the garage opened again and Mason stepped inside, sucking all the air from the room. I guessed his big head needed the extra oxygen to function.

"What's a nice offer?" he asked.

I rolled my eyes at his gruff voice and kept walking. "Nothing. I'll see you tomorrow."

He didn't respond, but judging by his narrowed eyes, he wasn't all that happy. But then again, I didn't think I had ever seen him so much as smile at me. He was happy-go-lucky with everyone else, but as soon as he saw me he went all frostbite.

He'd been around when I visited Willa at work before, and we've all gone out together a few times. He was hard to avoid; his brother was dating my best friend, yet for some reason, we always seemed to disagree about something.

I ignored his angry scowl and waved goodbye to Landon. I really had to hurry up, or Nora would think I wasn't gonna show.

The drive home was blissfully uneventful, and I made it with a few minutes to spare. I dropped all my stuff into Willa's apartment before going next door.

I opened the door with the key Nora had given me and was greeted by her three-year-old boy, Luca. "Esteballa, you are here," he yelled while dancing toward me wearing only his underwear and dinosaur slippers. I loved that he had a special name for me and secretly hoped he'd never be able to say my name properly.

Nora was a single mom who had been dealt a few blows in life, but she never let anything keep her down. I did what I could to help, especially since she had no support from her family or the kids' dad and was raising them by herself.

We met when I first moved in with Willa. I was heading out to meet Maisie and ran into Nora, who was struggling up the stairs with two kids and a bag of groceries. I gave her a hand and we bonded over our mutual love of unpronounceable cheese.

"Hey, bud, how was your day?" I asked.

"I gots to play with Pete t'day."

I kissed his chubby cheek and walked into the living room. "How exciting. Sounds like your day was more interesting than mine."

"Make yourself comfortable. I'll be right out," Nora called out from the bedroom. I plopped down on the couch and Luca threw himself next to me, a book already in his hand. He loved to read, and it was now our thing to read before we did anything else.

Nora worked nights at a bar, and I watched Luca and her little girl Lena a few times a week. It wasn't unusual for me to sleep on her couch because I was too tired to drag myself next door. We always joked that us meeting was fate.

"I might be a bit later tonight. We have a private function in one of the back rooms. Lena is already asleep. She didn't sleep much last night, so she was pooped," Nora said, dressed in her usual work outfit of skintight black jeans and a skintight corset. She refused to wear the short skirts that were part of the uniform, but she got away with it because she was a fantastic waitress and her boss loved her.

"You know I don't mind. It doesn't make a difference to me when you get home. I'll most likely be asleep anyway," I said.

She leaned over the back of the couch and kissed Luca's head, then mine. "I don't know what I'd do without you. Thank you for watching my babies."

"I love Luca and Lena more than anything. You know there's nowhere I'd rather be. Go to work already and leave us in peace. We have a few books to get through before bedtime."

"All right, all right, I'm leaving. Sounds like you have big plans. He's had dinner and a bath."

I waved at her, not looking up from the book that was open on my lap. "Not the first time I'm doing this. Go. We'll be fine. And I'll call if anything happens. Which it won't."

"Good night, baby," she called as she walked out the door, not waiting for a response. Luca was already lost in the book.

I squeezed him to my side until he started to protest. I wasn't kidding when I said there was nowhere else I'd rather be. "One book, then you'll have to put your pj's on, okay?"

"Two books," he bargained, knowing full well I'd agree.

"Fine. But no complaining when it's time to get dressed."

He held out his hand and we high-fived on it. Eight books later he was putting on his pj's.

Get Some Call It Temptation now.

OTHER BOOKS BY SARAH PEIS

Sweet Dreams Series

Some Call It Love (#1)

Some Call It Temptation (#2)

Kismet (#2.5) - newsletter subscriber exclusive

Some Call It Fate (#3)

Worship (#3.5) - only available in Sweet Dreams Box Set Part Two

Some Call It Devotion (#4)

Glamour (#4.5)

Some Call It Attraction (#5)

Spark (#5.5) – only available in Sweet Dreams Box Set Part Two

Sweet Dreams Box Set Part One

Sweet Dreams Box Set Part Two

Standalones

Adult Supervision Required

Contents May Catch Fire

ABOUT THE AUTHOR

I love the written word in all forms and shapes and if I'm not glued to a book, I'm attempting to write one. I'm a frequent blonde moment sufferer and still haven't figured out how to adult. Lucky google always has an answer, so I don't have to.

I live in Melbourne, Victoria, with my two kids, the holder of my heart and two fur babies. If you want to accompany me on my path to enlightenment, check out my publications or get in touch, I would love to hear from you!

WHERE YOU CAN FIND ME

Join my Blonde Moment Support Group (all hair colours welcome!) on Facebook to talk about blonde moments, parenting fails and of course books.

Facebook
Instagram
Pinterest
www.sarahpeis.com

THANK YOU

Thank you for reading this far,
    A legend is what you are.

There are so many people to thank,
    But when I get to this part I usually draw a blank.

Let's start with the beautiful Natasha who saved my characters from developing multiple personalities and traveling through time and space,
    You are an ace!

Ginna, I'll be forever grateful for your amazeballs support, you are simply the best,
    Thanks to you nobody will be hit with a cold bucket or suffer from a hot dog filled chest.

Robyn, there aren't enough words to tell you how much I adore you,
    One day we have to get a matching tattoo.

To my friends and family who support me in all that I do,

I f*ing love you!

Thank you to the wonderful Ben for creating a kick-ass cover design,

You really make my book shine!

Sim – I could never have done this without you, you are the love of my life,

I'm so proud to be your wife.

Made in the USA
Monee, IL
22 February 2024